Praise for *Switching Gears*

"An emotional tale of finding love after loss. *Switching Gears* boasts a cast of wonderfully flawed characters that grow their way into your heart."

—Kasie West, author of *The Fill-In Boyfriend*
and *P.S. I Like You*

"Packed full of competitive spirit and restorative heart."
—Natalie Whipple, author of *House of Ivy & Sorrow* and
Transparent

Praise for *Love, Lucas*

"Just as readers think they know how this story is going to end, a big plot twist changes the tale's course. . . . Fans of Sarah Dessen and realistic fiction with a poignant and sad slant will find this an enjoyable read."

—*School Library Journal*

"A deeply moving tale of unimaginable loss and the redemptive power of love. Sedgwick masterfully delves into the painful details of losing a loved one, breaking your heart even as her beautiful words stitch you back together. Romance and friendship, true growth and authentic healing, this story blew me away. It takes a special book to bring tears to my eyes *and* make me swoon."

—Rachel Harris, *New York Times* bestselling author of
The Fine Art of Pretending and *The Natural History of Us*

"Chantele Sedgwick's *Love, Lucas*, is a beautiful story about finding hope, first loves, and learning to live again after the loss of a sibling. With a fantastic cast, and the gorgeous setting of the California coast, this book is one fabulous read."

—Jolene Perry author of
The Summer I Found You and *Has to Be You*

"A beautiful, moving novel of loss and love. Sedgwick's elegant prose weave a heart-breaking tale that stays with you long after you have finished the last page."

—G. R. Mannering, author of *Roses* and *Feathers*

"An emotional summer of love, hope, and healing! Love, Lucas is easy to adore with Sedgwick's real relationships, sweet romance, and tale of renewal."

—Lizzy Charles, author of *Effortless With You*

"Chantele Sedgwick navigates the dark waters of grief with a deft hand and plenty of heart. *Love, Lucas* will drag readers under before bringing them back to the surface for a life-saving breath of hope."

—Amy Finnegan, author of *Not In the Script*

SWITCHING GEARS

CHANTELE SEDGWICK

Sky Pony Press
New York

Sky Pony Press books may be purchased in bulk at special discounts for sales promotion, corporate gifts, fund-raising, or educational purposes. Special editions can also be created to specifications. For details, contact the Special Sales Department, Sky Pony Press, 307 West 36th Street, 11th Floor, New York, NY 10018 or info@skyhorsepublishing.com.

Sky Pony® is a registered trademark of Skyhorse Publishing, Inc.®, a Delaware corporation.

Visit our website at www.skyponypress.com.

10 9 8 7 6 5 4 3 2 1

Library of Congress Cataloging-in-Publication Data is available on file.

Cover design by Georgia Morrissey

Print ISBN: 978-1-5107-0506-7
Ebook ISBN: 978-1-5107-0507-4

Printed in the United States of America

To my mom, Cheri Wardleigh
For teaching me to never give up and for never giving up on me.

"Biking is about rhythm and flow. It's the wind in your face and the challenge of hammering up a long hill. It's the reward at the top and the thrill of a high-speed descent. Biking lets you come alive in both body and spirit. After a while the bike disappears beneath you and you feel as if you're suspended in midair."

—*Gary Klein*

CHAPTER 1

Even after swallowing a bug about a mile back, I can't wipe the grin off my face. The breeze hums through the trees and rushes across my skin as I take the next turn.

The first mountain bike race of the season should feel different. After all those wintery months out of shape, I should feel more nervous. Anxious. Maybe a little scared. But as I shift gears to go up the last uphill before the end of the race, I'm elated. Higher than the moon, even. I was born to do this.

A mixture of pine and dirt reaches my nose and I take a deep breath, letting the fresh air in. I love the smell of nature. The trail is narrow here, with pine and fir trees surrounding me on both sides, but I don't feel claustrophobic at all. It's perfect—peaceful—and I wouldn't want to be anywhere else right now.

The climb is steep and my hands tighten on the grips of my handlebars. I'm sweating. I probably have disgusting sweat spots everywhere, but right now, I couldn't care less. The only thing between me and the finish line is this monster of a hill.

Uphill is pretty much my downfall, but I have a good feeling today. I've got a great lead. I can do this if I keep moving and don't lose my focus.

Almost there. Almost there. The thought keeps running through my head as I climb.

You've got this. You can do this. Keep pedaling and ignore the pain. Keep moving.

My sunglasses dig into my nose and I lift a hand to adjust them, wiping at the sweat pooling on my forehead. I wince at the burning in my legs, but they're nothing compared to my butt right now. It burns so much it feels like it's going to fall off. Which is a nice thought, actually, but the pain reminds me of how much I've slacked this season.

It's entirely my fault, of course. Mourning will do that to a person.

It's been a month since Lucas died. My neighbor, my best friend, and the boy I've loved since grade school. He's part of so many memories, and nothing I do can erase them. Which sucks. Sometimes I wish he'd get out of my head. That I'd forget him. But he just won't go away.

Instead of focusing on something else in my life, all I've been doing is, well . . . nothing. Moping, eating—pick something bad for you and that's me. But now, in the middle of this race, I feel a piece of me stitching itself back together. I've missed this.

All of it.

The dirt, the bugs, the pain. Everything.

I focus on the trail in front of me—keeping my breathing steady, feeling the familiar rhythm of my heart beat against my chest—and try and fail to keep thoughts of Lucas out of my head.

Nothing I do will change the fact that he's gone. I know that. But I can't help the way I feel without him here. Especially after he told me he loved me. I long for what might have happened if the cancer would have left him alone. He'd be waiting for me at the finish line right now. A huge smile on his face, and his blue eyes matching the sky.

I shake my head, cursing myself for the direction my thoughts have gone. Again.

Get your head in the game, Emmy.

I wipe the sweat from my forehead again and push on as the trail widens on either side of me. I've only gone a few more yards when I sense someone behind me. I frown and glance to my left as she passes me like it's nothing.

Whitney.

Her blonde ponytail flaps behind her as she passes me, not even looking winded, and to make things worse, she gives me a smug smile and winks. *Winks.*

My eyes narrow on her retreating back as the adrenaline kicks in and I push myself harder. I try to match her pace, but she keeps pulling further and further away. As much as I pedal, my lungs feeling like they're on fire, and I know it's not going to be enough. She's awesome and she knows it.

I fight to stay in control, my body protesting every single turn of my pedals, but my energy is fading. I had a great lead and I lost it.

Like always.

Whitney reaches the top and disappears for a split second. Once I reach it, I switch gears and pedal hard. The ground is flat up here and I ride on the smooth dirt until the downhill starts.

Rocks. Everywhere. I settle into a good pace, noting how far ahead Whitney is now, and start down.

I'm pretty good at downhill, but these rocks freak me out, so I'm careful not to hit one wrong. I really don't want to experience flying over my handlebars. Especially during a race.

The rocks get bigger the further I go and I maneuver the best I can, keeping up my speed, but cautious all the same. I can't remember the last time I had such a rocky downhill. This is definitely not my favorite trail.

I stand on my pedals and put my weight at the back of the bike, my butt a few inches off the seat. If you ever sit on a bike going down a hill covered with big rocks, I guarantee your butt will be black and blue. Even with the shock taking most of the impact, it still hurts.

A crowd cheers as Whitney passes the finish line and I try to stay upbeat. Second isn't that bad, but a frown creeps in anyway. She beat me.

Again.

I slide past the finish line a moment later and, despite the cheering from the people around me, I'm disappointed. I was sure I'd beat her this time. Sure of it. I pull on my brakes and roll to a stop, letting the dust settle around me. Whitney shoots me a smug smile as I unclip my shoes from my pedals and step off my bike, but I turn and ignore her.

My best friend, Kelsie, comes out of nowhere and tackles me in a huge hug. "Emmy, you did great!" Her momentum makes us both almost fall to the ground, but I catch myself on the guy standing next to us. I grab onto his arm, almost pulling him with us, but he flexes and I stand upright, still holding his arm. I glance up and give him a shaky smile.

I have no idea who he is and he's not very happy to see me. "Uh . . . sorry?"

He doesn't say anything, but shakes his head and walks away, leaving me staring after him with my mouth open. How embarrassing.

"That was awkward," Kelsie says.

I turn my attention back to her. "Yes. Yes, it was."

"At least he broke our fall." She giggles. "And you got second? Are you kidding me? That's awesome!"

"Thanks." I hug her back before pulling away from her grasp.

"Seriously. That downhill? Insane. And you, my friend, are insane for doing it."

I shrug. "It wasn't too bad. A little rocky." I smile at her expression.

"A little?"

"Okay, a lot. Kind of freaked me out for a minute. I kept picturing myself hitting one of the rocks and flying over the handlebars. That would have been lovely for everyone to see."

"I'm sure you would have been very graceful."

I laugh. "Thanks. I wish you could have raced with me today."

She shakes her head. "I know. My knee's still bugging me. Maybe next time."

"Next time for sure." I take a swig of water from my CamelBak. "Ugh. Warm."

"Warm water's the worst."

"I know." I take another swig anyway.

After I take my helmet off, I grab an elastic and pull my dark hair into a ponytail. My head is all sweaty and gross, which reminds me of the sweat stains again. I need to get in front of the air conditioner and fast. And then a shower would be nice. I feel bad for anyone standing too close to me.

"Hey, let's go get your time before we take off."

"Okay."

We walk over to the judge's booth and a man sitting next to a huge fan stares up at me. "Number?"

I look down at my jersey and the piece of paper pinned to it. "Twelve."

He nods, looks down at a piece of paper sitting on the table in front of him, and hands me an envelope with my number on it.

"Congratulations. You were second out of forty riders today in the sixteen to eighteen age group," he says.

Right. Second. And Whitney was first. Story of my life. "Thanks." I smile and take the envelope without looking inside. I already know what it is. My time and brochures for the next race. Second place doesn't get anything else.

"They'll announce the winners later on if you'd like to stay."

"Thanks." I turn to Kelsie. "Let's get out of here." I don't really want to stand in the heat forever just to hear my name announced. And I can't handle Whitney's gloating. To beat Whitney, I need to train more. If only I had a coach.

We walk to the parking lot and I put my bike on my rack. Once I lock it up, I hear music blasting through the parking lot. I don't even have to turn around to know who it is, but I find myself looking anyway.

Dirt flies up in clouds around his truck as he drives toward us, his music getting louder by the second. "What's *he* doing here?" I mutter under my breath.

"Seriously? Why wouldn't Cole be here, Em? The guys race at ten." She stands up straight and brushes her fingers through her light hair, giving herself a quick check in my side mirror. She looks at me and frowns. "You need to fix that hair. Stat."

"Are you kidding me right now?"

"What?" She takes a tube of lip gloss out of her pocket and slides it on her lips. "Cole's hot. Even *you* think he is. Don't even try to deny it either. I can see your lies coming a mile away."

"What does that even mean?"

She shrugs and reaches out to attempt to fix my hair. "Just admit he's hot. And put this on. Your lips are super chapped and need a little color." She holds out the lip gloss, but I don't take it.

I frown, knowing I won't win this one. Because she's right. He is. "He's also my least favorite person on the planet." I swipe her hand away from my hair and ignore the lip gloss in her hand. I don't have to attempt to look cute for anyone.

She sighs and puts the gloss back in her pocket. "No he's not. Whitney is. You're still mad the school mountain biking team picked him as team captain and not you."

"That's not the reason." I frown and avoid her eyes. It's totally the reason. We both know it. Obviously I haven't gotten over it.

"Pretty sure it is or you wouldn't be so defensive. *And* you'd still be on the team."

"Everything was fine until he had to take over. He's cocky, Kelsie. He knows he's good. He could lay off throwing it in everyone's faces."

She grins. "He kind of has a reason to be cocky. And honestly, he's not that bad. He was in one of my classes this year. He's nice."

"Nice? He's . . ." I try to search for the right word, but come up short. "Anything but nice."

"Because you know him so well, right?"

I don't say anything and don't turn to look at her glare.

"You know, if you'd get back on the team, maybe he could get some sponsors to watch you race. He had sponsors looking at him when he was in California. I'll bet they're still looking. He could totally hook you up."

"Doubtful. And Whitney would never let me back on the team now. She hates me."

"She doesn't have a say. You're the one who put the team together last summer, so everyone else's opinions would count more than hers."

"Still. I can't stand her."

8

She glances over at Whitney, who's busy flirting it up with a bunch of guys. "She *is* kind of a skank, right?"

I laugh.

"But in all seriousness. You should at least think about racing with the team again. You loved it."

"They don't need me when they have Cole. And I'm fine training by myself."

I don't miss her eye roll. "Sure . . ."

"Besides, I can't afford all the gear he wanted us to get. I can't even afford a pair of the gloves! He doesn't realize everyone doesn't have money like him. And the trainers he has? I'm not that good. I don't have anything else to offer that he hasn't already offered."

"Calm down. I know all the bells and whistles he has. I was on the team, too, remember?"

"You can actually afford things, though."

She shakes her head. "Not me. My parents. And you know they don't just buy me whatever I want. I have to work for it."

"I know. Sorry. I just . . . I wish things were like they were before he moved here." Like when life was a little less complicated. When I had more friends than Kelsie. When Lucas was still here.

Lucas. His name makes my stomach twist and my chest tighten. I wish he'd stop popping into my head all the time. It always kills my mood. I shake my head and focus on something else. Something that doesn't involve anything related to him. Like races and biking. Happy things.

"Well, they aren't. But we could make things work if you'd quit being so stubborn. Coach Clarke is trying to find some local businesses to sponsor the team, so the money thing isn't a good excuse. You need to let your grudge against Cole go."

I turn away from her and try to calm myself. She's right, of course. I have a hard time admitting defeat. Especially to someone like Cole. If there were such a thing as a playboy of mountain biking, Cole Evans would be it.

I haven't seen him since school got out a few weeks ago, but lo and behold, here he is. I was hoping I could avoid him until senior year, but I guess I'm not that lucky.

Cole pulls his black truck next to my wimpy car and rolls down the window after the dust settles. "Nice rack."

I roll my eyes. Even if he's talking about my bike rack, it still sounds ridiculous.

"Thanks," Kelsie says. "She just got it."

A high-pitched laugh echoes through the parking lot. I look over and see Whitney a few cars down. "That's for sure!" she yells and turns back to her friends to laugh some more.

My cheeks heat and I look away.

"I prefer Yakima, but Thule's pretty good," Cole says.

I turn to face him. "I only use the best."

His hazel eyes widen and he smirks, showing off the dimple in his left cheek. "Of course you do."

"What is *that* supposed to mean?" I put my hands on my hips and stare him down.

He raises his hands in defense. "Nothing, nothing. Just making conversation." He grins and I frown. I turn back around and shove my key into the bike rack to lock it.

Even though I already locked it. I just need something to focus on besides him.

"Is she always like this?"

Kelsie giggles. "Always."

"No, not always. Just when I have the pleasure of talking to you," I say. I don't look at him. I open my door to throw my gear on the front seat.

"Oh, come on, Marty. You're not still mad about the whole captain thing, are you?"

I cringe at both the memory and the nickname. "Of course not. The past is in the past." Even though I try hard to keep my voice even, it comes out clipped. "And don't call me Marty." My last name is Martin, but that doesn't give him the right to call me that.

I hear his truck door open and he jumps down in the dirt next to me. "But Marty's such a sweet nickname, isn't it?"

I turn around in a huff. "No."

He puts a hand on my car and leans toward me, trapping me in the corner of my open door. "So, what place did you get today? I'm assuming from the dirt all over your uniform that you raced?"

No. I rolled in the dirt for the heck of it. I grit my teeth. I really don't want to tell him. So I don't.

Kelsie steps in. "She took second."

His eyes widen, then he nods. "Not surprised. Congrats."

"Thanks," I mutter, knowing he'll get first in his division. He always does.

"Almost had first, right, Emmy?"

11

I glare at Whitney, who parks herself next to my car. She admires her nails and doesn't look up. "She was ahead the whole time and then lost it on that last climb. Too bad, huh?"

My hands clench into fists, but I keep myself under control. "I wasn't feeling the best today."

"Pretty lame excuse. You look fine to me. You're just not the best climber. Never have been." She smiles sweetly at me and I clench my fists tighter.

Cole must sense the tension coming off me because he ignores her and leans closer to me. "I can teach you to climb." His breath tickles my ear and I try to back away but have nowhere to go. "Just name the time and place and I'll be there."

I frown. "Um . . . no. Thanks, though . . . " *Flirting will not do anything for you, buddy.*

"Might do you some good," Whitney says. "Since you've kind of lost some of your A-game."

I whirl on her. "What are you talking about? I haven't lost—"

"I don't see you with a first-place medal around your neck." She chuckles and shoves her medal in my face.

"One loss doesn't mean anything."

She shakes her head. "This isn't your year, Emmy. It's just like last year. Get used to it." She turns and starts walking back to her friends. "You coming, Cole?"

"Just a sec," he says, searching my face.

I ignore the curious look he's giving me and try to push past him to . . . I don't know, make myself look cool and get all up in her face, but he won't move. And even as I push against his um . . . rather solid chest, I know I'm not going to get past any time soon. The boy's like a rock.

"It's not worth it," he says. "Settle it some other way. Violence is never the answer." His expression and voice is joking, but his eyes are serious. Why the heck does he care anyway? It's not like we're friends.

"I'll settle it right now," I snap.

Kelsie moves next to Cole. "Listen to him, Em. She's not worth it."

I stand there, unsure of what to do. I can't just let her walk away. It would be like backing down from a fight. And I don't back down from anything. "How about a rematch?" I yell before I can stop myself.

Whitney stops and turns around. "What?"

My heart quickens as I glance at Cole. He's staring at me, an amused expression on his face.

I glance away from him, flustered that he's so close. "I said," I draw it out just to be a jerk. "How about a rematch?"

She takes a defensive stance, crossing her arms and narrowing her eyes. "With who? Me and you?"

"Um . . . yeah? Who else would I be talking about?"

She stares at me a second and lets out a disgusted snort. "Seriously? You think you can beat me in a one-on-one race?"

"I know I can."

Cole chuckles and backs up a step, finally letting me past him. "I'd pay money to see this," he says, rubbing his hands together.

Whitney glares at him before looking back at me. "Fine. I'll play your little game. A rematch. Two weeks from now."

"Why two weeks?" I ask.

Whitney laughs. "So you can get some practice sessions in. You're gonna need them. I'd race you right now, but I don't want you to pass out or anything because you don't 'feel good.'"

I fold my arms and frown. I wish I could think of some witty comeback, but I'm at a loss for words right now. All I can think of is how much she looks like a Barbie with her bright pink spandex, helmet, even her bike.

Maybe this wasn't such a good idea. Who am I to think I can actually beat her? Especially when she's won every race the past year and a half. I have no chance. Even if I came in second today, she's still better.

"You having second thoughts? I would if I were you. Forget about the race, Emmy. You're obviously not in it to win it." She laughs as though she's just said the funniest thing in the world. "You ready to race, Cole? I wanted to watch you kill it out there." She smiles at him and I'm on the verge of punching her in the face.

Cole doesn't look at her, just keeps his eyes focused on me. "Come on, Emmy. I know you can do this. Don't you want to beat her?"

Yes. Yes I do. You have no idea how bad. I chew on my lip and can't help but notice his eyes shift to my mouth. I hesitate before I answer, wondering if there's any chance I could beat her. What if I *could*? I totally could. If I train hard every day for the next two weeks. Maybe?

"What do you say?" He's still watching me. Waiting for me to cave.

I let out an annoyed breath. "I'll race you," I say to Whitney.

She raises her eyebrows in surprise. "Really? You sure?" I fold my arms and nod and she kind of looks . . . impressed, maybe? Or maybe it's just my wishful thinking. "Okay, Emmy. Two weeks. What are the rules then? What's at stake?"

"Um . . ."

She snaps her fingers before I can say anything else. "I've got it. If I win, you admit I'm the better rider."

"That's not—"

"That's my only offer."

Of course it is. "And if I win?"

"You join your team again as captain, which I will happily give back to you," Cole says, answering for her. And by the look on her face, she's not happy about it at all.

"But—"

"On one condition. No more grudges. No more fights. The girls will be stronger with you on the team, Emmy. And you both know it."

Is he joking?

"Wait, what? No way. Not gonna happen."

He raises an eyebrow. "Are you always this stubborn?"

"Yes," Kelsie says, the same time I say no. "I'm trying to cure her of it, but it's not really working out. She's the worst."

"Traitor," I mutter.

15

Cole laughs. "Let's try this again then. If you lose, you admit she's the better rider, and if you win, we'll at least talk about you joining the team again. Coach Clarke has been hounding me to get you back. And if you come back, maybe I'll stop calling you Marty."

"Okay, enough chitchat. I'm bored. Cole," Whitney says, her eyes narrowing. "Let's. Go."

I ignore her and stare at him. "Really?" I'd really like him to stop calling me that. I don't like him. And for that reason, he doesn't have the right to give me a nickname.

"Really."

"Deal?"

He smiles as I reach my hand toward him. "Deal." His hand is warm and strong and tingles shoot through fingers all the way up my arm. We shake and I drop his hand and clear my throat.

Whitney glares at me. "If I were you, I'd get training. You have more work than you're cut out for if you want to beat me."

I fix my eyes on his, but answer her. "Bring it on."

Cole laughs. "I know an awesome trail you guys can race on in Park City. If you two are game."

"I love that trail. If it's the one I'm thinking about." She grins at Cole and nudges him with her shoulder. "Good memories."

His cheeks look a little pink as he avoids my eyes.

I don't even want to think about what they were doing on that trail. "I can handle anything she can."

16

He raises his eyebrows and gives me a sly smile. "Nice. Can't wait." He turns to Whitney. "I'm ready. Let's go. Later, Marty." He backs up, his eyes still on mine. He gives me a small smile and follows Whitney around the truck.

"What the heck was that about?" Kelsie asks.

I get in the car and she follows. "What do you mean?"

"He's totally into you."

I let out a snort. Super attractive. "Um . . . no. He likes tormenting me, that's it."

He did keep watching me, though. And actually tried to help me, which, from the way I've treated him in the past, I didn't deserve.

"Because he likes you."

"If he liked me, he wouldn't be with Beach Barbie."

She bursts out laughing. "I don't think they're dating, but she *was* wearing a lot of pink."

"That she was. The picture of her pink spandex butt is burned into my mind forever. I swear that's the only thing I see when I race anymore. Since she beats me *every* time."

"You'll get her in two weeks, Em."

"I hope so. Just once. I'd like to beat her just once."

I put the car in drive, leaving all thoughts of Cole and Whitney behind me. "Let's get a shake or something. I'm starving." Nothing like starting off the summer with a race and a nice yummy shake.

CHAPTER 2

After I drop off Kelsie, I head home. The results of the race eat at me again. I know I could have done better. I could have won. Things are going to be different next time. More training. Less thinking about Lucas and things I can't change. I don't care how hard it's going to be or how much time it takes. I'm going to get my life back, beat Whitney at our race in two weeks, and after that, I'll get first in my division. And maybe, just maybe, I'll agree to be captain and race for my school's team again.

Maybe.

My smile returns. I can do this.

I pull in my driveway, take my bike off the car, and roll it into the garage. I set it on my bike stand and start a mini tune-up before heading inside. I check the brakes and the tires for flats and assess the rest of it. The frame and chain are all dirty, so I grab an old towel and run it under the sink in the garage.

Have I mentioned I love my bike? No? Well, I do. I built it. I got the frame from a bike I found at a second-hand store a few years ago when I first started biking. It was in perfect condition. Not top of the line, but Trek is a good brand so I'm happy with it. It's white with black lettering, so I knew it would be a pain to keep clean when I bought it, but I didn't care. I was in love. Still am.

After taking a few classes on how to build and fix-up bikes at the bike shop down the street, I started buying some old bikes, fixing them up, and selling them to earn money to buy new parts for *my* bike. I'm really proud of my handiwork. I've replaced every crappy part on my baby with better ones. Brakes, gears, pedals, handlebars. Even the seat.

Now I'm kind of obsessed with it. Besides actual riding, fixing up bikes is kind of a passion. And as soon as I fix up and sell the two hanging on the wall above me, I'll have enough money to buy the new rims I've been saving for.

I wipe down the frame, rub the dirt off the pedals, and check out the chain. Dirty, but I'll clean it a little later. I don't realize how hungry I am until my stomach rumbles. I'm starving. Which is weird because I just finished a gigantic shake.

I shut the garage, grab my bag full of biking stuff, and trudge to the front door. I smell cookies when I walk inside and my mouth waters. I throw my bag in the corner next to the door and slip my shoes off before heading to the kitchen.

Mom and Dad decided to redo all the flooring in the house a year ago and both of them almost have a heart attack every time anyone forgets to take their shoes off before they walk . . . well, anywhere. You'd think they'd be a little less crazy by now, but no.

I chuck my socks up the stairs, hoping someone will get them to the laundry room before Mom sees them, and start down the hall. The hardwood floor is cold and feels good on my bare feet. I glance in the mirror as I pass the bathroom and my eyes widen at how crappy I look. Flyaway hairs are everywhere and I have dark mascara marks underneath my eyes. I look like a zombie who likes to wear spandex.

And people actually saw me like this? Nice.

When I walk in the kitchen, Mom's in her apron, her hair up in a messy bun. She has flour in her bangs, on her cheek, and across her chest. She pretty much always looks like that when she's been baking. She's not the tidiest, but she makes the best cookies around.

"Hey, Mom." I give her a quick hug, then sit down on a barstool and relax for a minute, drumming my fingers on the marble counter. I'm antsy. Not sure why.

I glance at the black-and-white cows decorating the room and hang my keys on the cow key-holder hooked to the wall by my head. Mom sure loves her cows. I usually have to warn my friends before they come over, because they're freaking everywhere.

"Where have you been?" Mom asks, running her hands under the faucet.

I shrug.

She takes in my outfit and smiles as she wipes her hands on a towel. "Biking again?"

"Where else?"

She chuckles but grows serious just as fast. "Were you alone?"

"No. Kelsie came with me. It was actually a race today."

Her eyes widen in surprise. "What? How'd you do? You should have told me. I would have come to see you."

"I got second."

"Really? That's amazing!"

She leans forward and hugs me, flour falling from her shirt onto my shorts.

I wipe the flour off and smile. "It wasn't a huge race. Not a big deal."

"Still. I'm proud of you. Next time tell me, okay?"

"I didn't think you cared about mountain biking."

She washes her hands in the sink and shoots me a grin over her shoulder. "I don't, but I like to support my daughter. Is that okay with you?"

"Yes. You're the best." Mom walks over and sets a plate in front of me and I pile a bunch of cookies on it. "And you made cookies for me, too."

"Technically, they aren't for you, but you can have a few." She grabs a glass out of the cupboard and puts it next to my plate. "There's milk in the fridge."

"Thanks. So, if the cookies aren't for me, who are they for?"

"A lady who comes in for prescriptions at the pharmacy every week or so." She pulls another cookie sheet out of the oven. "She needs a friend right now, so I thought I'd make her some cookies."

She's always thinking of others before herself. Even when she barely knows them. I need to be more like her. Care about more people. Especially ones I do know. "You're too nice, you know that?"

"Being nice isn't a bad thing, you know."

"Yeah, I know." I watch her roll more dough into balls and put them on a new tray. "Want to go to a movie later?

I know we couldn't do a girls' night last week, but there's a new chick flick playing at the theater. We could go if you're not busy."

She smiles. "That sounds fun. I'm sorry I had to cancel."

"It's okay." I say it even though I'm still a bit disappointed about it. We haven't missed a girls' night, or mom and me night, for years. Second Wednesday of every month since I was twelve. But conference calls and meetings with bosses can put a damper on things sometimes.

"I'll see what Dad's doing, but that sounds fun. I definitely need some girl time."

"Great." I take a bite of the cookie and chew. A strange flavor hits my tongue and it takes everything I have not to spit it out. I swallow as fast as I can and hurry to the fridge to grab some milk. I twist the lid off and pour it in my glass, downing most of it in a few gulps. I swish the rest, trying to get the gross taste out of my mouth. After I swallow, I lean against the fridge, watching Mom put another cookie sheet in the oven with her black-and-white oven mitts.

"Um . . . Mom?"

She turns, takes her mitts off, and tucks some hair behind her ear. "What?"

"Did you forget to put the sugar in the cookies?"

She frowns and glances at the plate on the table. "That's impossible. I know this recipe better than I know myself." She picks up a cookie and takes a bite. Her eyes widen as she chews and she leans over the garbage can to spit it out. She stares at the cookies, her hands on her hips. "I don't know what happened . . . I've never done that before."

I chuckle. "It's not a big deal."

"Not a big deal? I've wasted a whole batch of cookies."

I shrug and glance at the recipe book gathering dust on the counter next to the microwave. "I can make some more."

She frowns again, the crinkles near her eyes more pronounced than I've noticed before. She grabs a tray full of cookies. "You're not making more. It's fine," she snaps. She tips them into the trash can and mutters something under her breath. "Besides. You need to clean that mess of a room you live in." Then she frowns at my outfit. "And go change your clothes. You look ridiculous in those spandex shorts."

I stare at her. What the heck just happened? "Uh . . . thanks?"

She doesn't say anything else, just stands there, staring at the mixing bowl with a frown on her face. I wonder why she's so upset. They're just cookies.

"Here." I grab another tray and the plate off the table. "I'll clean up. Maybe Dad or Gavin can bring some pizza home."

She stares straight ahead and I'm not sure she heard me. "Mom?"

Still staring.

I touch her arm. "Mom?"

"What?" She's frowning at the garbage can now.

"I'll clean up for you. Go sit down. You look tired."

She closes her eyes and rubs her temples. "Sorry. I've been a little stressed out at work lately. Maybe I'll go take a nap or something."

"Okay."

She looks around at the messy kitchen and finally goes down the hall to her room. I finish cleaning up, call my brother to tell him to bring dinner home, and head downstairs to my room.

First thing's first: a shower and a change of clothes. My biking gear is fine and comfortable when I'm riding, but walking around in spandex for a while, especially in my padded shorts, tends to feel like I'm wearing a giant diaper. And . . . Mom's right. I do look ridiculous.

After a quick shower, I opt for my pajamas and grab a notebook when I'm changed.

If I'm going to beat Whitney, I have some training to do, but more importantly, I need to figure out *what* to do exactly. I try to start my list, but sit there, pen in hand, staring at the paper in front of me. I have no idea where to start.

So instead, I grab my iPod and stick the ear buds in. Nothing better than a bunch of girl music to get the ideas flowing.

After a while, I doze off. Until my older brother, Gavin, bursts into my room. He jumps onto my bed and knocks my notebook on the floor. Which, for the record, I haven't written anything in.

Gavin and I are only eleven months apart, but we couldn't be more different. I swear all he cares about is long boarding and work.

Long boarding is weird and I don't work.

Huh. Maybe I'm just a slacker.

"What are you doing in here?" I ask, ripping my ear buds out of my ears.

"Pizza's here." He tackles me and we both fall off the bed. "Mom told me to come get you."

"You're such a butt-head." I scoot away from him and stand, giving him the evil eye.

He snorts. "Seriously? Are you in third grade?"

I roll my eyes. "You're my brother. I can call you whatever I want."

"That's the best you could come up with?"

I glare at him. "Also, there's a thing called knocking. You can't just come down and barge in here whenever you want. I could have been naked in here."

He looks horrified and closes his eyes with his hand held in front of his face. "Fair enough." He grins and lets his hands fall to his sides. "For the record, though, Mom said I could come get you. She didn't say anything about knocking first."

"Of course she didn't."

He raises an eyebrow and swipes his light shaggy hair away from his eyes. "You two fighting or something?"

"No." I think about the cookies again. So weird.

Gavin sits down on my bed and looks around my room. "Lots of biking posters."

"You're very observant." It's not like I just put them up. They've been up forever. And he's been in my room before.

He chuckles. "Go on a ride today?"

"I had a race."

"How'd ya do?"

I try to smile, but the thought of Whitney winning makes it not as genuine. "I got second."

"Awesome." He hesitates a moment. "Did Kelsie race, too?"

I shake my head. "She's having problems with her knee, so no."

"Oh."

I'm beginning to notice something about my brother: I'm pretty sure he has the hots for my friend. Too bad that would be super weird. For me. They'd actually be kind of cute together. I stand and grab my dirty biking clothes off the floor to go throw them in the wash.

"So, do you want to come biking with me tomorrow? We'll go on an easy trail. Promise."

"Gotta work from eight till ten."

"Sounds awesome."

"I know. Lucky me."

"Well, when you're done waiting tables, you can come with me anytime you want."

"Nice try. I'll stick to long boarding."

"Lame. I don't know how you can do that. I've heard it's dangerous."

"And flying down the side of a mountain on a bike isn't?"

"Nope." I smack him on the shoulder as he rolls his eyes.

"We should probably go eat."

My stomach growls. "Yeah, probably."

We sit there for a second. He looks at the door, as do I. At the same time we run for it. I get to the stairs first, but as I run up a few of them, he grabs my foot and pulls me so I slide down three.

On my face.

"No fair! You cheated!" I catch up to him and knock him into the wall as he tries to pass me.

"Cheating isn't illegal when you're racing your sister," he says as I try to trip him. His footsteps are out of my reach and he bounds up the rest of the stairs, leaving me in a heap at the bottom.

I don't care if he's bigger than me. He's so going down.

CHAPTER 3

Saturdays are supposed to be awesome. And mine was, until about two hours ago. I put the key in the ignition of my stupid Civic again and turn it.

Nothing.

My car is officially a big piece of crap. And so am I, since all I have on me is a dead cell phone. Stupid battery. They've got to find a way to make phones last without batteries someday. But for now, I'm screwed. Without a phone. At the bottom of a stupid mountain, stranded in a dirt parking lot, and surrounded by a bunch of trees. Which are honestly looking pretty creepy as the stupid sun sinks lower in the sky.

And yes. *Stupid* is the word of the day.

This same thing happened last year, but Lucas was with me. His first ride. But he had a cell that actually worked.

We were at a different trail—an easier one, for his sake. I remember it was windy. Probably too windy to take a newbie biking, but he wouldn't let me reschedule. He was stubborn like that. Like me.

"You're sure this is as easy as you say it is?" he had asked as he stared down the dirt trail. His blue eyes were wide as he gripped the handlebars of his bike. He looked terrified, which kind of thrilled me. Just a little. He was always so good at everything he did, so I secretly hoped I could best him at this.

"You'll be fine. I promise. It's like . . . well, riding a bike." I tried to hide my smile, but it didn't really work.

He narrowed his eyes. "Really?"

I laughed. "Obviously. Just pretend you're on cement and you'll do great."

He sat back on his seat and squeezed his grips tighter. "I'm not on anything close to cement. I'm on dirt. Lots of dirt. With lots of rocks."

I glanced around. "There aren't any . . ." I trailed off as he pointed to a huge one in the middle of the trail. "Well, that one's kind of . . . out of place. But just go around it. You're a big boy." I patted his arm and he grinned. And I melted.

"Quit distracting me." He cleared his throat and flexed his fingers as a huge gust of wind came up. "This wind is totally throwing me off my game."

"At least it's not messing up your hair." I swear the kid had perfect hair. And I always let him know about it.

He let out a frustrated breath. "Helmet hair isn't any better."

"You ready? You look nervous."

He put a hand to his chest. "Me? Never."

He totally looked nervous. "You'll be fine. Promise."

"Whatever you say." He pushed off, going so slow that I had to control my laughter when we reached the next section of the trail. I pulled up alongside him as he stared at the downhill we were going to have to take. "There is no way I'm riding down that."

I snorted. "It's easy. I already told you not to pull your brakes too hard. Lean back on your seat and, most importantly, don't crash."

"Thanks for the tips, Miss I'm-way-more-awesome-than-Lucas." The sarcasm dripped off his tongue like water, but he couldn't hide his smile.

"You'd better remember that."

"Okay smarty-pants. You go first. I'll be right behind you."

"Great." I took off down the hill, relishing in the moment when all I could feel was the wind on my face. Once I got to the bottom, I stopped and turned to see where Lucas was. I tried to retain my laughter as I watched him walk his bike down the hill, but failed.

"Yeah, yeah. You kick my butt in mountain biking. I know. But I totally kill you in basketball."

"We're even then."

He smiled as he stopped his bike next to mine and leaned over to plant a kiss on my cheek. "Even if I suck, you're the bestest teacher ever."

My cheek tingled and I stared at him, losing myself in those blue eyes all over again. He had no idea how long I'd loved him, but there was no way I'd tell him. Unless he told me first. So instead of reacting, I giggled and tried not to let him see how much it affected me. "That was so cheesy it kind of made me want to barf."

He had acted hurt, but had burst out laughing two seconds later. "Me too."

The memory fades and I'm thrust back into reality. I feel the knot in my chest tighten and take slow breaths to keep myself under control.

With the door open, my eyes fall on the heart I had drawn in the dirt with Lucas's name in it. Why do I do this to myself? Emotion rushes through me as I stare at his name. I grab the stick I made it with and destroy any evidence of it being there.

I stand, chuck the stick across the parking lot, and sink back into the driver's seat. The knot in my chest loosens a little and I close my eyes and lean my forehead on my steering wheel.

Get a hold of yourself, Emmy.

It takes a few minutes to calm down. I've cried enough tears over Lucas the past year, and especially the last month, and I don't have any left. But still, sometimes they threaten and I have to fight to keep them at bay.

With a deep breath, I try to turn on my phone again before throwing it on the worn passenger seat.

My mom is gonna freak when she can't get a hold of me. Especially since I was supposed to be home an hour ago.

I've taken note of a few cars up here with mine, but Mom would murder me if I hitched a ride with someone I didn't know. I'm contemplating walking home, which would take for-freaking-ever, when Cole pulls up in his truck.

Perfect. Just who I want to deal with today.

"Everything okay, Marty?"

I look up, surprised at the concerned look on Cole's face. "Everything's peachy." Nice. I sound like Dad. Peachy? Really?

He looks at my car and back at me. "Car trouble?"

I sigh. "No."

"Hanging out in the heat for no reason then? Sounds like fun."

"It's a blast." I stare at the dirt again.

"Need a jump?"

"Someone already tried." Which is true. They even offered me a ride home, but I had to tell them no and I was too big of a wimp to ask to use their cell phone.

He gets out and leans against his truck with his arms folded. "Is someone coming to help you?"

"Yes," I mutter.

He raises an eyebrow. "Really?" He doesn't look convinced.

"I . . ." I sigh. "No. No one's coming. My phone died about two hours ago and I can't get in a car with a stranger. As much as I really wanted to earlier."

His eyes widen. "You've been sitting here that long?" He glances around before looking back at me.

I shrug. He's quiet for a moment and that's when I realize he's alone. He's never alone. "Where's your girlfriend?"

He looks confused. "Who?"

"Whitney."

He laughs. "She's not my girlfriend."

"Huh. Could have fooled me." I don't know why I even brought it up. It's not like I care.

"So . . . you're stranded up here." It's not a question.

I don't answer.

He lets out a breath and opens his passenger door. "Get in."

I glance up, surprised. "What? No!"

"I'm taking you home and we'll call a tow truck to come get your car." He moves toward me, his hand out. "Come on. I'm taking you home. I'm not a stranger, so you have no reason to refuse."

"Yes I do, I'm fine. And you're kind of a stranger."

He folds his arms again. "Seriously?"

I try to hide my smile, but I can't.

He doesn't look amused. At all. "Come on, Marty." He glances around and gestures to the setting sun. "It's getting dark. You're not staying out here by yourself."

"It's not that dark. And why are you up here anyway? You can't bike in the dark."

"Who said I was biking?"

I point to the bike in his truck. "Um . . . that?"

"That doesn't mean anything."

I let out a frustrated breath. "What are you talking about?"

"Sometimes I come up here to do a quick ride before the sun goes all the way down. I'm fine doing that. Because I'm a *guy*. Crazy stalker people won't bother me since I'm not a *girl*."

I sit up straighter. Who does he think he is? "You think just because I'm a girl, 'crazy stalker people' will bother me? I can handle myself."

33

He glares at me and folds his arms again. "Get in the truck."

"No."

He stares at me for a second, his jaw working. I've never seen him worked up before. "Come on, Marty. Get in the truck. It's not going to kill you."

"It might. And I'm not leaving my bike up here."

He throws his hands up. "Then unlock it and I'll put it in the back of my truck!"

I frown at him and twist the ring my parents gave me for my sixteenth birthday. "Tempting, but I'll pass."

"You're the most stubborn person I've ever met in my life," he snaps.

"Thanks."

His eyes narrow. "*Not* a compliment."

I stare at the ground again, wishing I were anywhere but here.

He sighs and I glance up as he rubs his temples with one hand. "Emmy, please. Let me take you home. I can call a tow truck on the way and come back with your dad or something."

My heart quickens as I realize he used my first name. He's never called me that before.

I chew on my lip and glance around. He's right. It *is* getting dark. And I've heard plenty of stories about the creepers that hang out in this area. I swallow my pride and take a deep breath. "Okay," I whisper.

"What?"

"You can take me home. And I don't need to call a tow truck. My dad and I can come back in the morning to get my car. This isn't the first time it's crapped out on me." I stand and wipe some dirt from my shorts. "This doesn't change anything, though."

He rolls his eyes. "Of course it doesn't."

I turn around to unlock my bike and I freeze as he reaches around me and takes it off the rack, lifting it into his truck.

"I'll lock it up if you want to climb in."

I stare at him for a moment and my mind goes blank as his hazel eyes search mine. He smiles and I look away. Instead of protesting the fact that he's man-handling my bike, I hurry and open my door to grab my purse before locking the car. I avoid his eyes as I get in his truck.

I'm flustered. And I don't like it. I clutch my purse tight in my hands. I'm shaking. I can't get a hold of myself.

Cole slides into the driver's seat a few seconds later and starts up his truck. He pushes on the gas and revs it a few times.

I glance over and hope he sees my annoyed look. "Do you really need a truck this big?"

He grins. "Bigger is always better."

I'm not amused. "I shouldn't have asked."

He shrugs and pulls out of the dirt parking lot.

I stare out the window as we drive down the mountain and away from my poor car. I hope no one steals it. Even though they won't, since it's obviously dead. It still makes me nervous, though, leaving it up here all by itself. We've been through a lot, that car and I.

But my bike is more important and I'm relieved it's in Cole's truck. It's worth more than my crappy car.

"Were you practicing for your race?"

"Of course." My voice holds back my nervousness. I'm not going to give anything away.

"I'll bet you were." He pauses for a moment. "You racing the Back Country next month?"

"Yep."

"Me too. There's supposed to be some sponsors there. Cool, huh?"

I nod. All I want is for a sponsor to notice me. Then I can afford some nicer gear. Maybe I could get those shoes I've been wanting. Or some new gloves that aren't so stiff.

We sit in silence. I pick at my nails; he taps on the steering wheel. I've never been good at starting conversations.

"Not a big talker?" I can hear the smile in his voice.

"Not really."

He chuckles and thankfully stops asking questions.

Before I know it, Cole pulls into my driveway. And that's when I realize something. "How do you know where I live?"

He reaches for the door handle. "Whitney lives around the corner. And I've seen you pull in here a few times."

"Oh." The thought of him knowing more details about my life is unnerving.

"I'll get your bike."

I nod and let myself out.

His muscles flex as he pulls my bike out of his truck. I can't help but stare and mentally curse myself for looking at all. Cole is not my friend. He never has been. He's my biking enemy. Nemesis. He took captain from me. I can't let him distract me and I won't fall for all of his charms like every other girl did our junior year of high school.

I'm sure he can't even count how many girls he's been with. I've heard so many rumors about him. Too many.

He holds onto the handlebars and pushes my bike toward me. "You sure you don't need me to call a tow truck? I can go back up and wait for them." He shoves his hand in his pocket and pulls out his cell.

I shake my head. "I'll do it tomorrow."

He raises an eyebrow. "You sure?"

"I think I can handle using a phone. And my dad has towing cables, so we're fine."

He frowns, puts his phone away, and takes a step toward me. I can't read the look on his face. "Why do you do that?"

"Do what?"

"Snap at me like that. When are you going to realize I'm not your enemy?"

I fold my arms and refuse to answer. I don't know. The fact that he took captain from me is a big deal. Not to mention, his bike is seriously worth way more than my bike and my car put together, which isn't hard, but still. He's all about money. If he can get the most expensive equipment, then he'll get all the sponsors. I know it's a stupid reason not to like someone, but I can't get over it.

"Thanks for the ride," is all I say.

"No problem." He takes a step back, and his expression is curious as he searches my face.

"What?"

"No more sarcasm? Really? You've been on a roll tonight."

I try to come up with something, but fail. "Well, fortunately for you, I've run out."

"Good news for me." He still stares, a smile creeping in as he tries to figure me out, I think. After a moment, he turns around and heads back toward his truck. He calls over his shoulder as he opens the door, "Later, Marty."

And just like that, my weird, confusing feelings evaporate. I'm still just Marty. Nothing more. I grab my bike. "Bye." I feel his eyes on me as I walk away and several thoughts fly through my head.

Stupid car. Stupid race. Stupid Cole. Stupid nickname.

CHAPTER 4

When my alarm blasts in my ear the next morning, I turn it off and make myself get out of bed. Most people would hit the snooze button, but I don't. The snooze button teases you with the notion of giving you a few more minutes of sleep, but then wakes you up five minutes later with no apologies.

I tend to avoid it at all costs. I don't like technology playing with my feelings like that.

Only when I'm halfway across the room do I remember it's Sunday. Which makes me wonder why the heck I set my alarm to wake me up so early in the first place.

Determined not to get up early, I get back in bed and snuggle in my covers again to try to go back to sleep. I give up after ten minutes. Unfortunately, I take after Dad. Once I'm awake, I'm awake for the rest of the day.

I drag my feet up the stairs, heeding the call of my growling stomach, to grab something for breakfast. I'm not surprised to see Dad in the kitchen eating Cheerios in his pajamas. His dark hair is kind of crazy and he's wearing his glasses on the edge of his nose while looking at yesterday's paper.

"Hey, Bug."

I roll my eyes. "Dad. No." He's called me that nickname ever since I was a kid, and no matter how many times I tell him not to, he does it anyway.

He takes a bite and looks at me thoughtfully as he chews. "Why are you up so early this morning? It's summer. You should be sleeping until ten like a normal teenager."

I smile. "Sometimes I wish I didn't have your genes."

He chuckles as he moves his spoon around in his bowl to get the last remaining Cheerios before looking up at me again. "You want to join me? There's plenty of cereal left."

I wrinkle my nose as he lifts the bowl to his lips to drink the milk. "I don't do Cheerios." Or drink leftover cereal milk. Gross.

He sets his bowl down and wipes his mouth with a napkin. "I know." He gives me a wink and stands to put his bowl in the sink. Once he's done, he looks at me again. "Hey. You okay? I mean, with everything that happened with Lucas . . ."

"I'm fine," I say a little too quickly. By the look he's giving me, he knows I'm not fine at all.

"If you need anything, let me know."

"Okay. Thanks, Dad." A sliver of light comes through the curtains and I peek through them. It's going to be a beautiful day. A little chilly this morning maybe, but nice. "Actually, I was wondering if I could borrow your car."

"Why?"

"I want to get a quick ride in this morning."

"You just went riding yesterday. Which, by the way, since we had to go get your car last night, I didn't get to bed until one."

"I know. And I'm sorry about that. Maybe you can just get me a new car?"

He frowns. "Nice try."

"Hey, it doesn't hurt to ask." I grin. "Please let me go. It will be a quick one, Dad. I promise.

"Emmy . . . Sunday's are family days."

Like we ever really do things together on Sunday. "I'll be back before Mom and Gavin wake up and we can do something then." I'm bouncing on the balls of my feet, itching to go outside before it gets too hot.

He stares at me a moment, leans against the counter, and rubs his hand over his face. I didn't notice before now, but he looks really tired. "Actually, your mother is already awake."

I give him a weird look. "Really?" Mom is notorious for sleeping in on the weekends. She's not someone I would call a morning person. Ever.

"We couldn't really sleep last night." He frowns and stares at nothing for a second before looking up at me again. "You know, why don't you go wake Gavin? We need to . . . have a chat with you guys."

"Really? You want me to wake Gavin up? This early?"

He smiles. "You can handle it. It will be good for him to get up early anyway."

"Okay . . .?" I frown as I walk down the hall to Gavin's room. Something's going on. There's no way Dad would

41

ever have me wake Gavin this early unless something's wrong. Did someone die? Grandma? One of the neighbors? He seemed a little anxious, but not upset. Maybe we're moving or something?

I don't bother knocking on Gavin's door, just let myself in. He's twisted in his blankets on the far side of his bed, his mouth open and drooling on his pillow. I can't *really* tell if he's drooling, but it wouldn't surprise me. I'm sure he's in his underwear under those blankets, so I avoid moving them at all costs.

I decide to be nice instead of jump on him, so I push his shoulder a few times. "Hey. Gav. Dad wants you up."

He rolls over, pulling the blankets with him. "Go away."

"Wow. That easy, huh? I was thinking of going to get a bucket of ice water to wake you up."

He frowns, his eyes still closed. "You'd regret it."

"Probably. Now get out of bed." I smack him on his bare back and he flinches. "Mom and Dad want to talk to us for some reason."

He yawns and opens one eye. "Do you even know what time it is? Or what day? I'm supposed to sleep in on Sundays."

"Of course I do. Now quit being lazy and get up."

He mutters a curse under his breath and wraps his blanket tight around him. Thank goodness. As he follows me out of the room, I can't help but smirk at how sweet his blanket cuddling is.

I glance over my shoulder at him and stick out my bottom lip. "Can't go anywhere without your wittle bwanky?"

He grumbles something I can't understand under his breath.

"Now who's the third-grader?" I add.

"Shut up."

We walk into the front room where Mom and Dad are already sitting on the couch. Gavin plops down on the floor and ends up on his side, half asleep and looking like a rolled-up burrito. His face is flat on the carpet and I wonder if there's any possible way he can be comfortable there. I step around him and sit in the chair, wishing I had a blanket. It's chilly this morning. I pull my knees to my chest and wrap my arms around my bare legs.

Dad's holding Mom's hand. She still in her pajamas, her hair pulled in a ponytail. She looks exhausted and I wonder why she doesn't go back to bed. She's obviously not getting enough sleep. Whatever they want to talk to us about must be pretty important.

"So?" I say, breaking the tension in the room. "What's up?"

Dad glances at Mom and she nods. "We . . . uh . . . I don't even know where to start."

"Start at the beginning then." Isn't that where you're always supposed to start when you tell someone something? And in this case, it's something big. I can see it in Dad's eyes. The nervous way they look at each other.

He glances at Mom again before he continues. "About six months ago, your mother started having some . . . symptoms. I don't know if you two have noticed, but she's been forgetful lately."

I remember the cookies, so I nod. And I guess there was that one time she forgot to pick me up at school a few months ago, but that wasn't too weird. I caught a ride home with Kelsie, so it wasn't a big deal.

"Well, one incident about three months ago finally made us go to the doctor to get it checked out."

"What happened?" I ask, glaring at Gavin, who's practically snoring on the floor. I kick him in the side, expecting him to yell at me, but all he does is turn over.

"She mixed up some medication at the pharmacy." My eyes widen. "Everything's fine, they got it figured out, but it could have been very bad for both parties involved." He gives Mom a small smile and squeezes her hand. "The doctors did some tests, and we've . . . well, we've known the results for a while."

"What? You've kept this from us for months? Why?"

"We didn't want you guys to worry. We weren't sure how bad it was. And at first, it wasn't bad. And as we think back now, she's had some of the symptoms even longer than six months."

I don't notice how tense I am until that moment. I adjust my position in the chair, letting my feet down to the floor, but still sit on the edge of my seat. "So, what's wrong?"

The worst possible things go through my mind. *Cancer. Heart failure. Lung disease. Stroke.* By the way Dad's looking at us, it's bad. But nothing prepares me for what he says.

He hesitates only a second before speaking again. "Mom has been diagnosed with early Alzheimer's Disease."

It's quiet. Dead silent. No one moves, no one speaks. I can't even think, let alone say something, and it takes me a few minutes to do just that.

Dad keeps talking, but I can't understand anything he's saying.

I open my mouth and close it and he stops talking and looks over at me.

"Emmy? Are you okay?"

"Alzheimer's? But . . . she's so young!" That can't be possible. Alzheimer's is for old people. Like my grandparents. And they don't even have it. How could Mom have it? It's not possible. I don't believe it.

He smiles. "I know. It is uncommon for someone her age, but not unheard of."

I look down at Gavin. His eyes are open and he sits up, but doesn't say a word. Just stares at the floor. For some reason I want to punch him. Make him do the talking instead of me, since every time I try to say something, emotion threatens to tear me open and let me bleed all over the floor.

Dad's watching me, concern etching his features. "We have some medication we're going to start, so that can alleviate some of the symptoms, but we do have to be careful. She's been in the early stage for a while now, but some of her symptoms are progressing into the middle stage, or moderate Alzheimer's. She's had some trouble remembering things, forgets where she is sometimes . . . we need to work as a family to protect her and make sure she's safe at all times."

I glance at Mom as a tear slides down her cheek and know I'm about to lose it.

She gives us both a shaky smile, all the while wringing her hands in her lap. Something I'd never seen her do before. She was never twitchy or nervous like that. "I'm going to be fine, you guys. They said the full effects of the disease may take a long time. Years and years. Don't worry, okay? I'm okay. If I do something out of the ordinary, talk to me. Bring me back. I know who you are and I won't forget you." She looks at me then, like she's talking to only me.

"You didn't tell us," I whisper. I'm hurt. Betrayed. My parents knew about this for months and never said anything? How could they do that?

"Honey," she says. "I didn't want you to worry. I still don't. I'm still your mom. I love you both too much to—"

"You kept this from us for six months?" I can't believe it. I thought we were a close family. We don't keep secrets like that. Why would they start now? What happened to break our family trust? Did I do something wrong? Did Gavin?

She sits up straighter and focuses on me. "We wanted it to be the right time when we told you. But there's not really a right time for something like this." She twists her hands in her lap, over and over and over.

I stare at them. I want to reach out and grab them, hold them still. "You could have told us right when you found out." I'm shaking. I'm not sure what I'm supposed to think. I don't know what to say to them. I can't even look at them. Especially Mom. All I know is that I need to get out of here. Now.

"I need to get some air." I stand and almost trip over Gavin's legs. I gather my bearings and walk past my parents, even as Dad protests. I run to the back door. I fling it open and hear it slam behind me as I run down the back porch steps and into the yard. I'm not sure where to go, so I run to the edge of the yard, sit down in the grass, and stare at nothing, breathing hard.

My body's still shaking. I'm fuming. Confused. Hurt. All my emotions are strung up in a knot in my chest and I can feel my heart breaking to pieces. I don't know how to stop it. I don't know what to do with it, so I sit there and shake.

The back door slams and someone heads across the grass toward me. It's Dad. I can tell by the way he walks. His right foot stepping harder than his left because of an old injury from his teen years. He hesitates only a second before he kneels down next to me and doesn't say a word. I feel his hand on my back and even though I try to fight it, try to ignore the fact that he's trying to comfort me, the tears come anyway. He puts his other hand on my arm and tugs. I only resist a moment before he pulls me into his chest and I sob like a little baby.

"It's okay, Bug." He strokes my hair and hugs me tighter. "It's going to be okay."

I don't answer. All I can do is continue to sob until I manage to get control of myself again. "How do you know? How do you know it's going to be okay?"

"I just do."

I pull away and look into his eyes. Dad has always been so strong. So wise. A perfect example of what a father should be. But in those eyes, I see doubt. I see the pain hiding underneath the surface. The reality of Mom losing her mind in the literal sense is hurting him, too.

"She's going to change. She won't be herself anymore." My mom. "She's going to forget us. Forget . . . me." The one person I can always count on for advice about anything. She's slipping away and I had no idea. I wonder how much she's already forgotten these first six months she's had this stupid disease. I admit I don't know a lot about it, but what I do know makes me shudder. People don't remember their own family members. Their spouses. Kids. No one. Sometimes not even their own names. I don't even realize I'm shaking my head until Dad grabs my hand, drawing my concentration to him again. "What am I going to do? What are *you* going to do?" I can't stop talking now. Even though I wish I'd just shut up. "What are we going to do, Daddy?"

His blue eyes swim with emotion and he squeezes my hand. "We're going to support your mother and treat her like we did before we found out about this. She's still here. She's fine. She understands what's going on, so we need to be here for her every step of the way when things start changing."

"She's never going to be the same, is she?"

Dad gets very serious and looks me straight in the eye. "No matter what happens with your mother, she'll always be the woman I fell in love with." He puts a hand on his heart. "Always."

CHAPTER 5

After talking to Dad, I retreat to the garage to work on one of my fixer-upper bikes. I need to clear my head. Do something instead of think and worry about Mom. The reality of it all is too much for me to handle right now. I can't accept it. Not yet. Maybe the doctor made a mistake.

First Lucas, now this? Why? Why is this happening to me?

I grab my hairspray bottle and spray a stream of it onto the bike's bare handlebar to attach the new grips I bought. I slide the right one on and then the left, making sure they're where I want them. I wheel the bike to the backyard and let it sit in the sun for a while. Hopefully they'll be good and dry by the time I get back from my ride.

After the events of this morning, I *have* to go for a ride. I don't want to sit around and sulk the rest of the day, and I'm kind of looking forward to getting away from my family for a while. Think about happy stuff. Avoid all thoughts of Lucas and especially Mom.

Right.

I run downstairs and change into my biking gear, taking extra caution to avoid Mom. I know she'll want to talk, but I'm not ready. She'll understand. I hope.

I sneak back upstairs, notice my stomach rumble, and grab an apple from the kitchen before I head back outside.

"I'm going for a ride," I yell, hoping someone heard me. If not, oh well. I already told Dad I was going riding earlier.

Thoughts from the morning's conversation come rushing back in as I put my gear in Dad's car, and my eyes water as I hook my bike up to my spare bike rack. The fact that my parents didn't tell me about Mom for six whole months makes me so . . . mad. I don't understand why they kept it from me. Or Gavin. I'd never keep something like that from them. There was a reason they did, I'm sure, but even if they tell me that reason it won't take away the hurt.

We're family. Why keep life-changing things from family? We're supposed to be there for each other to help get through things. Obviously my parents feel differently.

My hands hurt from working on my bike, but I shake it off and get in the car anyway. I try to tell myself to enjoy the mountain and not worry about anything else. Block out the crap life throws at me and I'll be happier. Pretend everything's fine, even when it's not.

My new motto.

Think about something else. Think about something else.

Cole pops into my head. Which isn't ideal, but better than the former. I do need to strategize, so I tell myself to make a plan. What would he do? He's the master biker. And he's offered to help, but I won't swallow my pride and ask him for help. Yet.

So, if I'm going to beat Whitney in our race and *then* in the Back Country race, the first thing I need to do is get rid of my distractions and focus. I'm going to need every bit of strength I have.

Don't think about Mom. Don't worry about Dad. Lucas is gone, so he shouldn't be a distraction still. Yet, he is. But not anymore. I'll forget about him, too. Block him out.

Distractions gone.

I dial Kelsie's number since I don't really want to be alone. She's probably in her pajamas still, but she's always up for a bike ride. I debate on telling her about my family and decide against it. I need some time to deal.

"Hello?" she answers with a yawn.

"You awake?"

"Kind of."

"Well, I'm coming to get you. We're going biking."

"Now? Do you know what time it is?"

"Yes. And I promise we'll go slow, since your knee is hurt and all."

She sighs. "Do you really need me to go? I'm still in bed."

I hesitate and can't believe I'm going to verbalize my next thought. "I'll owe you a shopping trip. Any time you want to go. And I won't even complain."

I hear her gasp. I never offer to go shopping with her. I loathe shopping. And she knows it. "I'll be ready in five." She hangs up and I smile.

Two minutes later, I'm sitting in her driveway. She looks like she's saying a few choice words as she makes her

51

way to the car. I get out and help her put her bike on the rack and we both get back inside and head for the trail.

"You're up bright and early," she says, sipping on a green smoothie. Her light hair is in a really messy bun and it looks like she's wearing the tank she slept in.

"I know." My fingers curl around the steering wheel and I focus my thoughts on the road.

"You okay? Usually you give me a heads up the night before if you want to go for a ride. Is it a code red or code blue?"

I smile. Red for broken heart or boy problems, and blue for family problems. "Blue."

"Ah." She nods and sips her smoothie. "Bad?"

"Bad enough."

"Want to dish yet?"

"Not yet."

"Fair enough."

The dirt parking lot is full of cars already, but I find a place to park. The only bad thing about the summer is how busy the trails are. Especially in the morning. The morning is the perfect time of day to ride. Not too cold, not too hot. But since everyone knows that, it can get crowded. I glance around at the cars again. We'll have to do a quick ride today, which is fine. I told Dad as much.

After we get our bikes ready, we head up the trail.

This particular trail is narrow most of the way through. Some of the trees even hang so low that we have to duck as we ride under them. And when there's someone coming the opposite way we're riding, we have to be really careful when we pass each other. You don't want someone falling off the side of the trail and rolling down the mountain.

I've seen it happen before and it wasn't pretty.

There are always more walkers on Sundays. Not sure why. Couples, groups, a few walking alone. The ones walking alone I like to stay away from because they're usually with dogs.

I'm not a big fan of dogs, especially in the mountains. They like to chase things. And those things are usually bikes. I'm typically okay with them, except for the people who walk their dogs without leashes. I've gotten chased, growled at, snapped at, and almost bitten more times than I can count, and usually the owners just smile and laugh as they apologize.

I don't think it's very funny, but whatever.

We ride for a while, enjoying the quiet, not pushing ourselves too hard, until we reach my spot.

I've been stopping at "my spot" since I started riding two years ago.

It's a giant, gray boulder that we have to jump to pull ourselves up onto. The view is amazing from here. You can see everywhere in the Ogden Valley below. A bunch of trees stretch out for about a mile, which then turns into houses peppered all across the valley, with roads in perfect squares as far as the eye can see. The roads let up around the Great Salt Lake if you look to the left of the valley, with Antelope Island looming in the distance. My favorite time of day to be at this spot is when the sun sets and it touches the water, but I don't come up too often around sundown.

I pull out my phone and take a picture. "Can you imagine what this would look like around Christmastime? I wish I could afford a snow bike. I'd ride up here all the time."

"Don't doubt it." Kelsie yawns and wipes some dirt off her shoe. Even after having only five minutes to get ready, she looks gorgeous as usual. Her hair may be a little windblown and messy, but her blue eyes are bright and her face doesn't show a trace of sleepiness. Me on the other hand . . .

"I bet we'd be able to see my house from here. Blinking like crazy with a zillion lights," Kelsie says.

I pull my knees up and wrap my arms around them. "Your dad is so awesome putting that display together every year."

"It's awesome, yes, but sometimes it's annoying. Especially when the lights keep flashing through my window every night. Makes it hard to sleep."

"Whatever. When I slept over last year in December, you were out in like two seconds."

She shrugs. "I guess I got used to it." She stomps her foot against the rock we're sitting on and mud flies everywhere. "Stupid mud."

"I told you to watch out for that puddle, didn't I?"

"Yeah." She frowns. "So, a code blue, huh?"

I shrug, wanting to tell her the truth, but not wanting to at the same time. I'm not ready yet. So, I take the easy way out and think of something else to tell her. Still the truth, just from another day.

"Yeah. It's nothing. You know how my parents get after me about me going biking all the time. It was one of those arguments." I force a smile as the lie rolls off my tongue.

"Sorry."

"And I think I'm just nervous for my race against Whitney."

"Don't worry. You'll kick her butt."

"Ha!"

"You can do it. You're just as good as she is."

"Come on, Kelsie. You know I have no chance. She's beat me every single time we've raced. And don't tell anyone I said that. Ever. It's not something I'm happy to admit."

She laughs. "Oh, I know."

"Even though I'd like to say I'm better, I know I'm not. I've heard she has sponsors looking at her. Real sponsors. I'd kill for something like that. I shouldn't have challenged her. What was I thinking?"

"She deserved to be challenged. And the only reason she has sponsors looking at her is because her parents are rich. Or maybe Cole has something to do with it. They seem to stick together, those two."

"I know. They're both rich, but they're both good. It's annoying." I frown and flick a little rock into the trees below us. "Have you seen Whitney climb? She's awesome. I get so tired going uphill."

"Yeah, but you kill it on the downhill." She laughs. "When there aren't huge rocks, I mean."

"No kidding."

She grabs a strand of her light hair and twists it around her finger. "But seriously. You scare the crap out of me with how fast you go sometimes."

"I like the thrill of it." I grin. "That sounded so stupid, but it's true." A few riders pass our spot, making me look up. "I wonder what time it is." I glance at my watch and frown. "We need to head down. My dad told me I could go on a short ride today. My parents will kill me if I'm not back on time."

I think of Mom and look out into the valley again as my mood darkens. I won't let it bother me. I won't. No feeling sorry for myself, and no crying.

Keep it together.

Kelsie plays with the bracelet around her wrist, looking thoughtful. "So . . . how's Cole?"

"What do you mean, *how's Cole?*"

She chuckles. "I love how riled up you get the second I mention his name."

"I do not."

"Do, too. Do you know what I think?"

"No. And I don't really want to know either."

"I think you two would be so cute together."

"Oh, come on, Kels—"

"Just think about it. You're a mountain biker, he's a mountain biker. You could totally get married and have mountain biking children."

"You're super hilarious."

"A family of mountain bikers. It's like your perfect fantasy."

I try not to smile, but I can't help it. Even if what she's saying is totally ridiculous, she always knows how to cheer me up. "Whatever."

She puts her arm around me. "He's into you, girl. And I'll prove it."

"Don't. Please. I don't need you to play matchmaker."

She laughs. "Oh, I'm not planning on being the matchmaker. You two will do that on your own. There's so much chemistry there. I just need to give you guys a little push." She smiles and I feel my cheeks heat.

"I don't like Cole."

"Just keep telling yourself that. Have you ever noticed how he always seems to find you? And by the way he teases you, it's totally obvious. Teasing means he likes you. And with how sarcastic you are with him . . ."

"Kelsie, I don't like him." I grit my teeth. I can't like him. He's not Lucas. I stare out into the valley, my whole body tense. "I barely know him at all."

She unwraps her arm from around my shoulder. "You're still not over him are you?" She gives me a small smile and puts a hand over mine. All I can do to keep from crying is shake my head. "Oh, honey. I'm sorry." She's quiet, gathering her thoughts while I try to push mine away. "It's okay to move on, you know? He'd want you to do that."

"We should go." I sniff, scoot away from her, and jump down from the rock.

I hear her following me, but she's quiet. I feel bad now. It's not like I don't want to move on. I do, I just . . . can't.

Kelsie glances at me as she slides her gloves back on. "Hey. I'm sorry. I shouldn't have said anything."

A long sigh escapes my lips. "You can say whatever you want, Kels. I know you're right. I just don't want to admit it, you know? I'm having a hard time letting go."

She nods. "I know." She gets back on her bike and adjusts her helmet. "So, to cheer you back up, I have a proposal for you."

"Shoot."

"Breakfast. Tomorrow. Then we go to the mall and get some shopping done."

I squeeze my eyes shut, the thought of shopping already giving me a headache.

"Hey. You promised."

"I know."

"Want to race back down?"

"Right. Have you seen this trail? It's super narrow. We'd totally take each other out and run over all the walkers on the way."

"Yeah. You're probably right."

"Let's do it anyway." I push off and hear her laughing behind me.

CHAPTER 6

I don't do Mondays.

And since I hardly slept at all last night, I'm basically a well-dressed zombie sitting at breakfast with Kelsie. We started the tradition last year with our biking team—breakfast at our local diner every Monday during the summer. Now it's just me and her. We should start a different tradition, but I like scones too much.

Today, though, even scones can't pull me away from my bad mood.

I stare at the old records hung up on the walls and wonder what it would have been like to live back in the fifties. I wonder if life was as complicated as it is now. As I contemplate changing the song on the awesome jukebox in the corner, I'm certain of one thing: things were a lot simpler then.

I wonder how I'd look in a poodle skirt . . .

"Emmy." I glance up as Kelsie nearly finishes off her scrambled eggs and looks at my plate. "You haven't touched your food. What's the matter?"

"I'm tired. And I'm not feeling too great." I still haven't talked to Mom. I shut myself in my room all day yesterday and then left before she got up this morning. Maybe that's why I don't feel good. The guilt is starting to eat at me.

She frowns. "You could have texted me this morning. I would have brought soup or something over instead. Even though soup would be gross for breakfast." She shivers and takes one final bite of scrambled eggs.

I take a tiny bite of my scone and chew it up before pushing it away. "Soup can't cure what I have."

"Soup can cure anything. Especially mine."

"Yours comes from a can."

She shrugs. "What can I say? Campbell's has healing properties."

I roll my eyes and stare out the window. "All I have is a headache. Not a big deal." I swirl my eggs around on my plate as I eye my scone again. I may have to take it home.

She sets her fork down. "Seriously, though. What's up?"

"Nothing."

Her eyes narrow. "Something's up. You're my best friend. I can read your moods better than I read my own."

"Is that even possible?"

"Of course." She downs her orange juice in two seconds and sets her cup on the table. "Want to tell me what's bothering you? You look . . . worried or something."

I shake my head. "I'm fine, Kels. Really. We have some stuff going on at home, but it's not a big deal."

"The same thing as yesterday?"

"I don't really want to talk about it right now."

"Okay. Anything I can do?"

"Not right now." I smile to reassure her. "But thanks."

"Hey, Kelsie, Marty."

I look up and see Cole striding toward us. He's alone again. No Whitney or his other biking minions.

"Hi," Kelsie says.

I don't say anything, just fight the urge to get up and leave. After our encounter in his truck on Saturday, I really don't want to talk to him. Even though it wasn't really an "encounter" at all. He was being nice and giving me a ride home. I don't like the way he made me feel, though. All flustered.

Stupid boys.

Cole stops and folds his arms. I have to admit, he looks good this morning. His green shirt brings out flecks of green in his hazel eyes. I look away to stop myself from checking him out further. "Still do breakfast every Monday?"

"Yep," Kelsie says, finishing off a piece of toast.

"I thought so." He looks at me. Something like regret flashes across his features. "Want to get some practice in after breakfast, Marty? I'll meet you in Ogden if you'd like. Give you some pointers."

I frown as I look at him. "You keep asking me that. Why would I need pointers from you?"

"You know why." He grins.

I lean back against the booth and fold my arms. "Maybe if you didn't have that ridiculously large ego, I might actually say yes."

"Really?"

My eyes narrow. "No."

He laughs. "Fine. Just thought I'd offer since you don't have a car right now."

My face heats. I never told Kelsie about him taking me home and even though she's trying to look like she's super interested in what's left of her breakfast, she's listening. "I'll . . . uh . . . get a ride with Kelsie if I go. Thanks, though." I shift uncomfortably as he stares at me.

"Sorry, Em. I have to work. Remember?" Kelsie winks and stands up and leaves me. "I need to wash this syrup off my hand. Be right back."

Syrup? Really? She didn't even have pancakes.

Cole smiles after her, then slides in next to me, his arm resting on the booth behind me. He leans close, and the near contact makes my heart freak out. "So, is it really a no? I'd rather go with you than by myself. If you're up to the challenge."

Is he asking me out? No. Never. Even though a part of me—a very small part—maybe kind of wishes he was.

"I have stuff to do." I glance at him, keeping my face as straight as possible. "Thanks for the offer though."

The corner of his mouth turns up. "You're using 'stuff' as an excuse to not hang out with me? Ouch."

A smile tugs at my lips. "No. I really do have a bunch of stuff to do. At home. For my family." I grimace. "You know . . . cleaning and stuff."

Cleaning and stuff? You couldn't have thought of a better excuse?

Someone calls Cole's name and he turns as one of his friends greets him from across the room. He raises a hand at him and turns back to me. "Well that sucks. Okay. Maybe we can do it again sometime. When you don't have

62

to clean and stuff. See you around then, Marty." He tugs on a strand of my hair, grins, and walks away, leaving me confused and flustered. Again.

"So . . . what's this about him knowing your car is dead?"

I glare at Kelsie as she slides back in her seat. "Thanks for leaving me."

She chuckles. "Just letting you guys have a moment. So, spill. I know you have some details you're not telling me."

I sigh. "My car died at the trailhead the other night and . . . Cole showed up. He took me home. No big deal."

Her eyes widen. "No big deal? This is huge! And a second ago he was totally asking you out."

"Was not." I look over as he sits down next to one of his friends in another booth. He glances at me, catches me staring, and sits up straighter with a smile on his face. My cheeks burn as I turn and stare at my food.

"Was too. Didn't you see the way he was looking at you?" She pauses. "The way he's still looking at you?" She chuckles as I glare at her. "There's something there. He wouldn't have asked you out otherwise."

I grit my teeth and push my food around my plate. "He might have asked me to go riding, but that doesn't mean he was asking me out."

"Oh, quit being so . . . *you* and let the guy take you out."

"I'm not going out with him, okay?"

I don't mean to snap at her, and as soon as I do, I feel horrible.

She's quiet for a moment and instead of finishing her breakfast, pushes it away. "Sorry, Emmy. Didn't mean to make you mad. Is this about Lucas again?"

"No. It's just . . ." I think of Mom again and shake my head. "My family. It's kind of got me on edge. I'm sorry for freaking out. I really didn't mean to take it out on you, I swear."

She shrugs. "You're allowed to have a freak-out once in a while."

That earns a tiny smile from me, but I'm still not happy.

"I'm here if you need to talk about it," she says.

I sigh. "I know."

She's silent again, but perks up fast. "Why don't we do something to take your mind off everything?"

"Like what?"

"What are you doing tonight?"

I scan my mental list of things to do. Besides working on bikes, it's blank. I sigh. I don't have a life. "Nothing."

She frowns. "I thought you had stuff to do?"

My lips twitch and I fight back a smile. "I thought you had to work?"

She chuckles. "We're horrible liars."

"Yes. Yes, we are. So, what's the plan?"

She takes a bite out of *my* scone, chews, and swallows before talking again. "Sorry. It looked really good."

I wave my hand. "You're fine."

She shrugs. "I know. Anyway, I have a few ideas. And none involve shopping, believe it or not. We can do that tomorrow instead. I can tell I'd be pushing it if I took you today."

"I'm fine."

She gives me a pointed look. "Sure. Anyway, I'll narrow my ideas down and we'll do something awesome."

"Okay . . ." I try to look super excited, but in actuality, I'm super scared.

Kelsie's ideas of fun are way different than mine.

CHAPTER 7

Mom and Dad are gone when I get home, so I hang out in the garage and try to fix up the Gary Fisher I've been working on so I can put it online and try to sell it.

The bike is in pretty good shape. And after finding it at the second-hand store for ten bucks, I'd call that a steal.

Normally when I fix up a bike, I can sell it for at least triple what I bought it for. Like the Scott I sold last week. Bought it for $15 at a yard sale, fixed it up, and sold it for $150 online. People don't know how much bikes are really worth when they just throw them out like that.

I grab a bottle of blue nail polish and cover up some of the scratches on the bike's frame. It's almost a perfect match. From far away, no one could tell it was a little off.

A good thing about fixing up old bikes is I now have a huge stash of every color nail polish I'd ever want. Sometimes when I go to the store, I'll buy ten different shades of blue, come home and match it to a bike I'm working on, and take the rest back the next day. The checkers always look at me weird when they see the receipts I bring back. At least they know I'm not really a nail polish hoarder, though.

I glance up as Gavin comes through the garage door. He has his car keys and is dressed in his work clothes. "Hey, Gav."

"Hey." He grabs the brake on the handlebar closest to him and smiles. "Having fun?"

"Sure."

"I was wondering . . . since you haven't said much about . . . you know. About Mom and all that." He frowns. "You doing okay?"

I glance up at him, seeing the concern on his face. "I think so."

"Good. That's good. I'm heading to work, but if you need to talk, you know where to find me. I know how you like to handle things on your own. But it's not good for you. So, just know I'm here. Waiting to talk when you're ready. Okay?"

"Thanks, Gav." I reach out to give him a hug, but he makes a face and puts his hands up to stop me.

"Are you kidding? There's no way you're hugging me when you look like that."

I glance down at my outfit covered with grease stains and chuckle. "Fine." I put my arms down. "Have a good day at work."

He nods, gets in his car, and drives away.

I kind of love my big brother. Always looking out for me, even when I don't realize it.

Once he's down the street, I turn on some music and smile as it blasts through the garage. Our neighbors probably hate me. I hum along to the song as I reach for the bowl of vinegar the cassette is soaking in and smile as I see all the flakes of rust settling at the bottom. Vinegar does wonders. I pull out my old toothbrush and scrub at the few flakes left.

While I scrub, thoughts of Mom take over. I wonder how she's doing today. Maybe I should ask her if she wants to go out to dinner and . . . talk or something. I want to know things. I want her to tell me how she's feeling and how things are affecting her and how badly. I want to keep doing our girls' nights without worrying if she'll remember them or not. I know I should keep treating her the same—like nothing's wrong—but I can't when I know there *is* something wrong. And what if she doesn't *want* to talk to me about anything? It's not like she came out and told me what was going on anyway. I shake my head and focus on the task at hand.

I take out the cassette, look it over to make sure I didn't leave any rust in any crevices, and set it on a towel to dry. The vinegar is gross and smelly on my hands, so I stand to wash them.

As I do, someone pulls into my driveway and my mouth drops open as I realize who it is.

Cole.

He smiles when he sees me and jumps down from his truck. It takes five seconds to realize I'm wearing an ugly pair of pajama shorts and an old faded tank-top. My hair is in a messy bun and I'm sure I have grease stains on my face.

I have to talk myself out of running inside and changing.

"Hey," he says as he walks up to greet me. His eyes take in my awesome outfit, and I see the corner of his mouth twitch.

"Uh . . . hi?" I'm standing with my hands outstretched, soaked in vinegar, and I'm pretty sure my mouth is still hanging open. I glance down at my outfit and feel my face heat. What a wonderful time for him to show up when I look so amazing.

His smile widens, and I really want to say he looks like crap, too, but no. He's wearing his biking gear and looks . . . hot. Yes. I said it. And right now I kind of hate myself a little.

I hesitate a second more before I'm coherent enough to say something. "What are you doing here?"

He shrugs. "Just finished a ride and thought I'd come say hi." He glances at the bike I'm working on and raises an eyebrow. "Isn't that bike a little tall for you?"

That snaps me out of my staring. "It's not mine. Well . . . technically it is, but I'm not going to ride it. I'm fixing it up to sell it." I leave him standing at the edge of the garage and go wash my hands in the sink hooked to the back wall. When I return to the bike, he's checking it out.

"You fix these up?"

"Yep."

He looks up at me and I swear I see a flicker of amazement cross his features. "That's . . . awesome. Did you build your own?"

"Yes."

"Sweet." He glances at my bike sitting a few feet away and then back at me. "I ride but don't build. Maybe you can teach me a few things sometime."

"Okay." I stare at him, wondering what he's really doing here. "So, all you came to do was say hi?"

"No, not really."

"Oh?"

He plays with his keys in his hand and looks kind of nervous. "I was wondering if you and Kelsie wanted to get some friends together and come bowling tonight."

I stare at him. "Are you serious?" I can't remember the last time I went bowling. It's been years. And believe me when I say I'm super awesome at it.

Total lie.

He shrugs. "My cousins are coming in from California and I'm supposed to entertain them tonight. I thought it would be nice to invite more people. Mainly, you and Kelsie."

"Why?"

He smiles. "Is it a bad thing to want to hang out with you?"

My cheeks heat and I grit my teeth together. I don't know why he has to do that. Make me feel all . . . fuzzy. Fuzzy? "I'll . . . uh . . . talk to her, I guess."

"You guess?"

"Yes." I sit down in my chair again and think about what else I need to do to the bike in front of me. Distract myself. From him.

"You're not going to come up with a stupid excuse like earlier today, are you?"

I glance up at him. "Huh?"

"I invited you to go biking, but you said you had stuff to do. Like cleaning around the house."

I shrug. "I do."

"Cleaning bikes around the house?"

I blush. "Exactly."

He raises an eyebrow and gives me a half smile. "Whatever you say." He waits for a moment and I can feel him watching me. "So, you game?"

"For what?"

He lets out a frustrated breath. "Bowling."

"Oh. That." I stop what I'm doing and look up at him again. "I'll think about it."

He smiles. "Great. We're leaving around six tonight and meeting at West Point Lanes. I'll probably have to drive my cousins, so meet us there?"

"Sounds good."

"Great." He backs up, his eyes never leaving my face. "See you there, Marty."

I cringe at that. "We'll see, Evans."

He laughs as he gets back in his truck and drives away. I stare at it until he turns the corner.

What just happened?

CHAPTER 8

I stare at the bowling alley in front of me and frown. "No."

"Come on, Emmy. It'll be fun," Kelsie says.

"No way."

"Cole's waiting for us. We're late. His cousins are going to be disappointed if he doesn't bring friends. He told me to come in and find them. They're at lanes 7 and 8."

I fold my arms and lean back against the seat. "I didn't realize you'd been fraternizing with the enemy behind my back."

She laughs. "Fraternizing?"

I shrug and give her half a smile. "It seemed like a good word to use."

Kelsie chuckles. "If you come, I promise I'll make it up to you. You know, for all my fraternizing."

"How?" She'd better do something awesome. Like letting me off the hook to go shopping with her.

"I'll buy you a shake on the way home. Caramel brownie. Your favorite."

A shake. Such a trivial, fattening thing. But one of the only things she can use against me.

Curse you, food, and all of your deliciousness.

"Fine," I grumble. "It had better be a large."

She laughs. "Of course you'll do it for food."

I frown. "It's my weakness. I can't help it."

"I still can't believe you can eat like you do and still stay that size," Kelsie says.

I grimace. "It will catch up with me, I'm sure."

"Doubtful." Kelsie helps me out of the car and links arms with me. "Thanks for coming with me. I know we're gonna have fun. And just because I love you, I'll throw in a side of fries with your shake on our way home. Deal?"

"Might be pushing it," I say. "I'm supposed to be eating healthy. You know, the whole biking thing?" I frown. Maybe that's why I can't beat Whitney. Maybe I should start nibbling on crackers all day instead of downing a shake in five seconds.

"I'll eat some, of course."

"Fine."

"Look. I told you I wanted to help take your mind off whatever was bothering you, so here we are."

"You should have told me we were coming here, though. I would have passed."

"Is it helping?"

I let out an annoyed breath. "A little." It's true. I haven't thought about Mom since we got here. Until now, I guess. But I'm sure when I'm actually inside with Cole and his friends, it will be the furthest thing from my mind. I can hope, at least.

"I knew this would work. You should trust my judgment more often."

I sigh. "I know."

When we walk through the doors, hot, stale air hits me. It smells like old shoes and grease.

Which makes me think of my closet first, and then for some reason, bacon.

I'm kind of hungry. Maybe I shouldn't have skipped dinner.

"There they are. Let's hurry and pay and grab our shoes before we head over," she says.

We walk up to the register and Cole meets us there. "Marty, you made it!" He glances at Kelsie. "You're awesome, you know that?"

She grins. "I know."

I shoot Kelsie a look before glancing at him. "How many games are we playing?" I dig in my purse, but he's already pulling out his wallet.

"I'll pay for these two," he says to the worker.

"You don't have to—"

He's already getting change back. "Thanks," I mutter. He really didn't have to do that. Now I owe him. I hate owing people things.

"What size shoe?" the worker asks.

"Six."

Cole laughs. "Are you kidding me? You only wear a six? Your feet are tiny!"

A slow smile creeps to my face. "Not really, but thanks. I think."

"Miss Tiny Feet," Kelsie grumbles as she picks up her size nines.

We share clothes all the time, but shoes? Never.

"We're just finishing putting everyone into the computer," Cole says as we follow him over to the two lanes he's reserved.

My favorite person in the world is typing in the names on the board. And for once, she's not wearing pink. Whitney immediately frowns when she sees me, but it disappears just as fast when Cole starts talking to her.

"Add Kelsie and Emmy, Whitney."

"Sure." She shoots me a smile and puts Kelsie in. Then she adds me, but instead of my name, she puts an E and tells me she accidentally pushed enter. "Sorry," she says.

I shrug. "No big deal." What I really want to do is tell her where to stick her stupid E.

As I glance around the group, I notice besides Whitney and Cole, all of the friends he invited are other bikers. They were all on the team together last year. My old team. Mark, Isaac, and Jamie sit across from me, and John is taking his turn.

I notice two girls standing near Cole, both with dark hair and tanned skin. The older one, or at least taller one, looks over at me and gives me a smile. She says something to her sister—I assume it's her sister since they look almost exactly alike—and leaves Cole's side to walk over to me.

"You must be Emmy," she says, holding out a hand.

I take it. "Yes. I'm Emmy."

"I'm Mia. Cole's cousin. That's my sister, Madison." She gestures to her sister, who smiles and gives me a small wave before sitting in one of the seats. She looks a bit paler, I mentally note. "It's nice to finally meet you. I've heard a lot about you today."

My mouth drops open slightly. "Really?"

"Sure. Cole told me how awesome it is to know a girl who's so good at mountain biking. He didn't know many in California, so it's new for him."

I blush. "Oh. Thanks."

"Seriously. Take it as a compliment." She smiles as Cole calls her name.

"Mia, you're up!"

"I'd better take my turn. I don't even know why he makes me bowl at all. I'd do just as well sitting over here. I'm horrible." She chuckles and walks away.

As she goes, Mark takes her place beside me.

"How's it going?" he asks. He takes a seat and brushes his jet black hair across his face. "I haven't talked to you in forever."

"I'm good. You?"

"Great. You ready for Back Country in a few weeks? It's supposed to be killer."

I nod. "Looking forward to it. Why haven't I seen you at the last few races?"

He shrugs. "I've been out for a few months. I crashed and dislocated my shoulder. It's on the mend, but it's still bugging me."

I shiver. "Sounds painful."

"Not too bad. But bad enough to have to let heal before I ride again."

"Kelsie's knee is still healing as well. She can ride, but she has to go pretty slow. Hopefully you can ride again soon too."

"Planning on it."

"Hey, Mark. It's your turn," Whitney snaps.

He gives me a small smile before he stands and leaves me alone.

"He's a cutie," Kelsie whispers.

"He really is." I actually had a crush on him last year, but then he started dating a girl from a different school. I wonder if they're still together.

Mia sits next to me again and we relax in comfortable silence, cheering everyone else on. She was right when she said how horrible she was. She bowled a 1 on her first turn. I'll probably match her or get worse.

Once everyone else but me has taken their turn, Kelsie stands to take hers. Of course she gets a strike on the first try. She's a natural at every sport, I swear.

She squeals and hugs everyone on the way back to her seat. "Want to put a bet on this game?" she asks when she plops down next to me.

"Um . . . no. I'll be happy if I bowl a 20. I suck."

She laughs. "You said it, so I can agree with you."

"Thanks for that." I give her a smile as I walk up to grab a bowling ball to take my turn, but as I'm standing there on the slick floor, my phone rings. I pull my cell out of my pocket and frown. It's Mom. I stare at her name flashing on the screen. She doesn't usually call me unless there's an emergency. I turn around. "Kelsie, why don't you go for me. I need to take this." I push answer and start walking outside so I can hear her better.

"Hello?"

"Emmy?"

"Hi, Mom. Is . . . everything okay?"

She's silent for a moment, which makes me nervous.

"Mom?"

"Oh. Hello?" she asks. "Who is this?"

"It's Emmy."

"Oh, honey, is something wrong? I thought you were out with your friends tonight? Why are you calling me?"

My eyes burn and I have to bite my lip to stop from crying. She's fine. She's just a little confused. Maybe I really did call her. My phone was in my pocket. I could have butt-dialed her accidently and she's calling me back. I try not to panic and make sure my voice is steady when I speak. "Um . . . I wanted to say hi. See how you were doing."

"Oh, good. Where did you go again?"

"Bowling."

"That's right. Dad told me. You winning?"

"No."

"I haven't been bowling in years. We should go some-time. Maybe in a few weeks for girls' night. Does that sound fun?" She's quiet again and I shiver as a breeze touches my bare arms. "Emmy? You there, honey?"

"Yes."

"Don't worry about calling to check up on me, okay? I'll see you when you get home."

"Okay."

"Love you, Em."

"Love you, too."

I hang up and stare at my phone for a long time.

CHAPTER 9

The day Lucas told me he had cancer again was a lot like this. It was one of those times in which I couldn't do anything to change the situation and ended up crying for hours after. I had known something was wrong. He hadn't been his usual self for a few weeks, but no matter what I said, he'd shrug it off and act like everything was fine. I knew my best friend, though. He was just . . . off.

It was late. Almost eleven when I got his text. All it said was that he would meet me out back. I slid off my bed, told my parents where I was going, and went outside. I'd met him in his backyard so many times, I knew I'd find him sitting in his parents' porch swing as I hopped over his fence.

"Hey," I said, putting my phone in my pocket and sitting next to him. "What's up?"

He leaned his head back, his eyes on the night sky. "Sorry it's so late. I just . . . it's been a really crappy day."

"I'm sorry. Anything I can do?"

He shook his head. "No. It's nothing you can fix."

"Okay?" He was scaring me. There was obviously something very wrong. I could see it in his eyes.

"Em, I need to tell you something. It's pretty big. And I haven't told anyone yet."

My heart sped up. Whatever he was going to say sounded bad. "What's wrong? I can tell something's been bothering you for a while now. Are your parents okay? Is Oakley okay?"

He smiled. "My sister's fine. So are my parents. For the most part anyway."

"Oh. Good." I folded my arms and shivered at the slight breeze.

He was quiet for a moment. A few crickets chirping somewhere in the yard was the only sound in the starry night. It could have been the perfect moment, but then he spoke. "My cancer's back."

My world crashed down around me as I sucked in a breath. "What?" It came out as a whisper on the breeze.

He closed his eyes. "I've been really tired and weak lately and have had a lot of pain. So we went to the doctor a few weeks ago. It's bad." He opened his eyes and sat up to face me, taking my hands in his. "Em, I'm not gonna make it."

I dropped his hands. "What do you mean, you're not gonna make it?"

"The cancer's everywhere. They gave me six months. Tops."

This couldn't be happening. This was Lucas. The guy who beat cancer once. The boy I was in love with. He was strong. He could fight this.

I was shaking. My eyes burned. And when he scooted closer and put his arm around me, I leaned my head on his shoulder and let a few tears fall.

He pulled me closer. "It's okay, Em. I'm not afraid of dying. I accepted it a long time ago."

"How can it be back? You beat it. You're perfect now."

"It's just my time."

"It's not fair. You're too young to die." I wiped at the tears trailing down my cheeks.

He chuckled, the rumble in his chest making my heart constrict. "No one's too young to die. Some people aren't really ready for it, but you can't stop what's meant to happen. And I've accepted my fate. I'll be okay."

"I won't."

He squeezed my shoulder. "Thanks for always being there for me, Em. I don't know what I'd do without you. But you'll be strong. You have your family. Oakley. Kelsie. You'll manage without me."

I wasn't sure what I'd do without him. The thought of him dying was more than I could take. "How's Oakley?"

He sighed. "Not good. Give her a few days before you try to talk to her about it. She's taking it the hardest."

"Okay." She'd been distant lately, that's for sure. Now I knew why.

He sat up a little straighter, but didn't move his arm. "Let's not talk about depressing things anymore, okay? I'd rather just sit here and enjoy the quiet. The stars are bright tonight. It's . . . calm. I need calm right now."

"They are bright." I wiped my eyes and, as I moved my hand back down toward my lap, Lucas grabbed it and linked out fingers together. He didn't say anything. He didn't have to. All he needed was someone to sit with him and be there for him while he dealt with everything.

My mind was going crazy, though. Did anyone else know? His friends? His girlfriend? She didn't deserve him. She never had. And how was I supposed to watch him get weaker and weaker until he disappeared into nothing? I wanted to scream. I wanted to punch something. I wanted to curse every disease capable of taking those I loved away. But I didn't. I relished in the moment of Lucas trusting me enough to tell me what was going on. And sitting in that porch swing that night was a memory I'd cherish forever.

When I got home later that night, Mom was waiting for me. I didn't even know she was there until she flipped the lamp on. One look at my tear-streaked face and she was on her feet.

"Honey, what's wrong?"

"His cancer's back." I couldn't say anything else, just sobbed as she pulled me close and stroked my hair.

She was quiet, listening to my sobs and crying silently herself. No words about how everything was going to be okay or how Lucas would win his fight. No false hopes. And I loved that about her. She just let me cry. She was just there. My rock. And I knew she'd be there for me every other time I would need her.

But now, my rock was slipping away. And oh, how I needed her.

CHAPTER 10

I don't know how long it's been when Cole finds me, but I'm sure it's been a while.

"Hey," he says as he sits on the curb next to me.

"Hey." My tears are dry by now and hopefully my face isn't red, but I'm sure it's a little blotchy.

Dumb emotions. I hate crying.

"I wondered where you ran off to. You okay?"

I nod. Just feeling sorry for myself and thinking about things I can't change.

"You sure?"

"Yes." I rub my arms, and before I know what he's doing, he shrugs off his dark jacket.

"Here."

"Oh, no, I can't take your—"

"No worries." He puts it around my shoulders and I give him a shaky smile.

"Thanks." It smells good. Like cologne. I try not to let him see me breathe too deep. That wouldn't be awkward at all.

"So . . . you kind of disappeared. Kelsie has been bowling for you."

"I'm probably winning then?"

He chuckles. "She's pretty good."

I nod. "I know. She puts me to shame at everything."

"Besides mountain biking?"

"I guess. Are your cousins having fun?"

"I think so."

"That was nice of you to take them out on the town."

He chuckles. "Not much to do here, but bowling works, I guess."

"Are you guys close?"

"We get along, yes. My mom and their dad are siblings. We don't see them a ton, but they do come around sometimes. When they do, we have fun. They're only in town for a few days this time, though. Madison has an appointment with a specialist here. She has a kidney disease and she's not doing very well. They're hoping this doctor has better news than her other ones."

"I'm sorry."

He shrugs. "Life. If anyone can deal, it's Madison. She's the most positive person I've ever met. Mia, on the other hand, she's convinced she'll be able to donate a kidney to her when she turns eighteen. I hope she'll be able to. For both their sakes."

"Me too." I think of Lucas when he got his diagnosis. I squeeze my eyes shut as my eyes start burning.

He's quiet for a moment. "You ready for your race next week?"

"Yes." I like one word answers. They're short. And about all I can handle right now.

"Really?" He raises an eyebrow and gives me a small smile.

"Yep."

"I believe you. I've seen you ride, you know. You're good."

I didn't expect that. "Thanks."

"I wish you'd reconsider and join the team again."

"I don't think so."

He sighs. "Look. If there's anything I can do to change your mind, tell me. We could really use you. Our scores could use a boost. Especially against that team from Layton. They almost had us last week. It would be good to have another person who knows what she's doing."

I shake my head.

"I figured you'd say no."

"What's that supposed to mean?"

He shrugs. "From past experience, I know you won't change your mind no matter what I say."

"How do you know? You don't even know me."

"I'm trying to get to know you. If you weren't so stubborn, we'd be past all the small talk by now."

I don't know what to say to that, so I just sit, staring at him with my mouth open. Why does he want to get to know me? We're two very different people. He's the laid back, not a care in the world type and I'm . . . the opposite.

He's watching me and I avoid his eyes. I'm not sure what he wants or how I got myself into this situation. I shouldn't have come.

"You're really hard to read, Emmy."

My name on his lips makes my heart speed up. "Thanks . . . I guess."

He shrugs. "I can usually read people pretty well. But you? You're different."

"Oh." This conversation keeps getting more awkward and I'm really wishing Kelsie would come find us.

"You're still mad about me taking over captain."

"You won it, fair and square." It comes out clipped, even though I try to keep my voice steady and indifferent. "The team chose you and not me."

"And that hurt you." He hesitates. "I'm sorry. I shouldn't have taken it from you. It wasn't my place."

I stare at the ground. I wasn't expecting him to apologize, especially for this. "No." I look up at him with half a smile. "You're the better choice. You've had professional coaches and know a lot more about it than I do. I'm just a . . ."

"A what?"

I let out the breath I'm holding. "I don't know what I am."

He doesn't say anything, but I do see his hand lift up a little, like he's going to put his arm around me or something. Part of me wants him to. "You're awesome at fixing up bikes."

I chuckle. "I guess so."

"And you're a pretty amazing rider."

I shrug. "Sometimes."

"Not sometimes. You're awesome. Especially for someone who taught herself how to ride."

"Thanks . . ." This conversation is kind of freaking me out. I glance at him out of the corner of my eye. "What do you want, Cole?"

He stares at me. "What makes you think I want something?"

I ignore that. "You just . . . you usually don't go out of your way to talk to me. And the past few times we've seen each other, that's exactly what you've done."

"You read into things too much. And I don't want anything. Like I said before. I'm trying to figure you out."

"Why?"

"Because you're interesting."

"Cole, please."

He grins. "What? You don't believe me?"

"No."

"Why not?"

"There's no way you're interested in me."

He smiles. "I never said I'm interested in you, just that you're interesting."

I swear my whole body blushes. I'm such an idiot. "I didn't mean—"

He scoots a little closer so our legs touch, which makes me all kinds of nervous. "What if I am?"

I stare at him. "Am what?"

"Interested in you." He lets it linger in the air for a moment and I can't look away from him. His eyes slide over my features and I shiver. "Normally a guy would give up on a girl who tried to insult them every time they were around, but not me. I know there's more to you than that. I watched you last year. And not in a creepy way, I swear. I've just noticed things. You're loyal to your friends. You care about people you love, more than you care about yourself. When I first met you, you were very friendly and welcomed me into your group even though you didn't know me at all. I haven't forgotten that." He smiles and then his face grows serious and he frowns. "But then I took captain from you and something changed. And I'm sorry. I made you hate me before you even got to know me."

I want to tell him it's not all his fault. Maybe a tiny bit, but when Lucas told me his cancer was back, that did it. It changed my outlook on everything. It changed me. "It wasn't you," I whisper.

"Then what was it?"

I don't want to talk about Lucas right now, so all I do is shake my head and play with the ring around my finger.

"It's because of that boy, right? The one who died a few months ago."

My heart feels like it might stop as the breath whooshes from my lungs. I don't answer, just keep twisting my ring around my finger.

"I didn't know him, but I heard he was a good guy. Were you two close?"

I bite my lip and give a slight nod. "Yes."

"I'm sorry."

I shrug. I don't know what else to do.

He folds his arms and stares into the parking lot with me. Voices echo from the bowling alley. People laugh, bowling balls crash into pins. It's so loud in there. Chaotic. It's just as chaotic in my head.

"So I was wondering something."

I jump as his voice pulls me out of my stare. "Okay."
Hopefully he changes the subject.

"What are you doing Friday night?"

I lean away from him as my eyes grow wide. "Cole,
don't."

"Why not?"

"I . . . you have a girlfriend."

"Last time I checked, I didn't."

"What about Whitney?"

"What about her?"

"She likes you."

"So? I don't like her. Like that anyway."

"You two had a fling or something, though."

"I wouldn't call it a fling. She was nice to me. And I
could tell she kind of liked me. When you're new to a
school and don't know anyone, you attach yourself to the
people who accept you. After hanging out with her a few
times, I realized she wasn't my type."

I bite my lip. "What about the other girls?"

"What other girls?"

I laugh. "People talk. I'm not going to be like every
other girl at our school."

His eyes narrow and he clenches his jaw. "You believe
everything you hear?"

"Ever since you came here, all I've heard are rumors.
Who you've been with, and whatever else you like to do."

"Been *where* with?"

I sneak a look at him and he's grinning. "You know
what I mean."

He laughs. Loud. "That's pretty funny. And the key-word for tonight? *Rumors*. Not truths. Just because I'm nice to people doesn't mean I'm some player who sleeps with every girl he meets."

"There wouldn't be any rumors if you didn't."

He smiles. "Everyone has baggage, Emmy. Even you, I'm sure. And rumors don't do anyone any favors."

"Do truths?"

He shrugs. "Depends on the truth."

"Tell me a truth then," I challenge. "So I know what to really believe."

"Why should I?"

"Because apparently all I know are rumors."

He studies me for a long time before leaning in and tugging on a strand of my hair. "I kind of like it that way." He lets go and leans back again, still watching me.

I let out a frustrated breath. "What is the point of this conversation then?"

"Does there have to be a point to every conversation?"

I glare at him. Same old Cole. I do have an opinion of him. Jerk.

But now I'm curious. Curious to what truth he's hiding from me. From everyone. I look over at him to find his eyes on me. Challenging me.

The thing is, I don't have a clue what to say.

"You're tongue-tied. That doesn't happen very often, does it?" He smiles, his face inching toward mine.

"Uh . . ." He's right. I am. I blink once. Twice. What am I doing? What's wrong with me? I hate the fact that I'm letting my guard down around Cole, but it's totally happening. And I'm terrified.

"Emmy?"

I shoot to my feet as Kelsie comes outside. "Hey." I tuck my hair behind my ear and step away from where Cole's still sitting.

"You okay?"

"Yes. Just . . . talking."

She gives us both a strange look and I swear she's trying not to smile. "Okay. I'll go back inside then."

"No!" I don't mean to shout, but I do anyway. I give Cole a nervous look, but all he does is smile. It's more than a smile, though. Like borderline laughing. "Um . . . I'm ready to go."

"Now?"

"Now. I . . . uh . . . need to get home. My mom was on the phone and needs me."

She gives me the *I know you're lying, but I'll listen to you anyway* look. "Okay. You might want to go return your bowling shoes before we leave. I don't want you to go all klepto on me."

I slip them off my feet and start to walk inside, but she grabs them from my hands. "I'll grab your shoes. Be back in a sec."

She goes back inside, leaving me alone with Cole again.

"So, everything's not okay. If you're leaving so soon," he says.

I bite my lip.

"If you ever want to talk, let me know."

I turn to look at him and he looks so . . . concerned. He takes a step closer and reaches for my hand. It takes all I have in me not to pull away.

"I'm fine."

"You don't look fine. I know for a fact you were crying out here earlier."

Curse my blotchy face. "It's not a big deal."

"It obviously is."

"Why won't you let this go?"

"Maybe I want to help."

My temper picks up again and I pull my hand away from him. "Maybe you should learn to mind your own business."

He takes a step closer, a frown on his face. "Maybe you should learn how to be nice to people who care about you."

"The only person who cares about me is Kelsie."

"Maybe because you're rude to everyone else who tries to care."

"I am not."

"Prove it then."

I fold my arms and back away from him. "Just . . . leave me alone."

He stares at me for a second, his eyes so serious, and opens his mouth to say something else when Kelsie walks back outside.

"You ready?" She hands me my shoes.

I nod and slip them on. I feel Cole's eyes on me as I shrug off his jacket and hand it back to him. "Thanks.

For . . . inviting us tonight. Sorry you wasted your money on me." I meet his hazel eyes for a second and look away.

"Money well spent."

I look up and meet his gaze once more. His stare is kind of intense and I have to tell myself to keep breathing. I'm still mad at him. Mad at how he makes me feel. Confused.

"We'll have to do this again," Kelsie says.

He breaks eye contact and smiles at her. "For sure. And maybe you won't even have to drag her here next time."

She puts an arm around my shoulders. "I hope not."

"We'll see you two later then." He rocks back on his heels and shoves his hands in his pockets.

"You, too." Kelsie turns me around and walks me to the car.

"Bye, Emmy."

"Bye."

My stomach does a flip and I link my arm through Kelsie's.

"You're blushing," she says.

I crack a smile. "Shut up."

CHAPTER 11

The ride home is quiet. I lean my head against Kelsie's window, thinking about my conversation with Cole, then thinking about Mom's phone call. She called *me*, right? I pull out my phone and make sure. Yes. She called me. Her symptoms can't be bad already, can they? I swear Dad said she was on medication that would help her.

I should ask him. I should talk to her. Ask questions.

But I can't. Not yet. People her age don't get Alzheimer's disease. It's for old people. Not for mothers with teenage daughters. It has to be a mistake.

A huge mistake.

"Hey," Kelsie says, making me jump. "You kind of disappeared tonight."

"I know. I'm sorry. Thanks for taking me home early." I grimace. "Sorry about that, too."

She's quiet for a moment. When she speaks again, she's careful. Hesitant. Like she could shatter me into pieces with her words. "You know I'm here for you, right?"

Tears prick my eyes as I stare out into the dark. "Yes."

"You want to tell me what's going on?"

I take a deep breath. Kelsie won't tell anyone. I trust her more than anyone in this whole world. So . . . I tell her. Everything. "It's my mom." She waits, doesn't rush me, just keeps driving. "She was diagnosed with early Alzheimer's six months ago. My parents just barely told me."

Her mouth drops open just enough for me to notice. "Oh, honey, I'm sorry."

I don't talk. I can't. Just stare out the window into the dark. The houses become blurs as my eyes well with tears and I blink really fast to make them go away. I'm not going to cry again. I already made a mess of myself earlier. So much so that Cole even noticed.

I'm such a baby.

"Is there anything I can do?"

"No. I mean, I'm fine. And for all I know, she's fine. Dad says she's . . . I don't know. She's okay. She has a few memory lapses sometimes that make things interesting." I take a slow breath. "I can't . . ."

I shake my head and stop talking, emotion overwhelming me. She's okay. I have to keep telling myself that. Maybe she won't get any worse. And maybe if I don't pay too much attention, I won't notice if she *does* get worse. I'll remember the good times. The normal times.

The times when we'd stay up all night talking about Lucas or when she'd check me out of school to go get a pedicure when she knew I was feeling down. She always knew how to cheer me up. Always knew exactly what to say. I don't know if she'll be like that in a few months or even a few weeks and I can't watch her deteriorate like that.

"Well, if you need anything, let me know." She turns the corner to go to my house, then about throws me out of my seat as she flips the car around.

"What are you doing?" My fingers dig into the sides of my seat. I swear I can feel perfect indents of my fingers already there from all the times Kelsie has almost killed us in her car. She's crazy. And I'm pretty sure she has road rage.

"I forgot. I owe you a shake and some fries. And after this conversation, I'm buying you whatever else you want."

I chuckle. Right. "Of course. You know the way to my heart. Thanks, Kels."

"And you need to tell me what you and Hot Stuff were talking about."

"Hot Stuff? Really?"

She laughs. "Oh, come on. You were thinking the same thing. I saw how close you two were. I even stood by the door for a sec to see if you were gonna get closer." She wiggles her eyebrows.

I bury my face in my hands as she laughs again. "For the last time: I don't like Cole," I mumble. Even though the way he held my hand those few seconds kind of . . . I don't know. Changed things a little. But I'm not about to admit that. I'm still in love with Lucas. I can't fall for someone else.

And what did he say? I'm rude to everyone? Am I?

"Did you have fun tonight?" I ask her.

"Yes. I did. I kicked everyone's butt."

"Of course you did."

We're both quiet and, as we glance over at each other, we burst out laughing. My night feels a lot lighter than before.

I don't know where I'd be without my Kelsie.

CHAPTER 12

Morning wakes me bright and early and I'm secretly happy I'm the only one awake. I change into my biking clothes, throw my hair in a ponytail, and creep upstairs to make a morning green smoothie. Of course the blender decides to crap out on me, so I make a ton of noise pushing the fruit to the bottom with a knife and shaking it around to get the blender to work. I pour out my brownish icy goodness and gulp it down.

Time to start eating healthy if I want to kick Whitney's trash.

"Hey, Bug."

I jump and spill some of my drink on my jersey.

Nice.

"Oh. Hi, Dad. What are you . . . why are you up so early?"

He looks at me like I'm an idiot. "I leave for work at 6:30 every day."

Of course he had a reason to look at me like that. "Oh. Right." I set my cup in the sink and hurry and fill my CamelBak. I suck a little of the leftover water from my last ride out to start the flow and spit it in the sink before draining the rest and filling it back up with new water.

Dad's hovering behind me, but I don't turn back around. "What are you doing up so early this morning?"

"Uh . . . just keeping busy. Doing . . . teenager things."

"I'm pretty sure getting up at six in the summer isn't a normal teenager thing to do."

"Yeah, probably not."

"Going biking today?"

"Yep."

"You know, you've been living on that mountain lately. I'd like to see my daughter every now and then."

I turn around and smile. "You're seeing me right now. And you saw me yesterday. And the day before that."

He frowns. "You know what I mean. I'd like to actually spend time with you. And not just to pick up your broken-down car." His stare makes me feel guilty that I've been avoiding everyone.

"Sorry. I've had things to do. I'll try to be around more." I know I won't.

"Honey, if you need to talk about things, you know I'll listen. And Mom, too. She's been worried about you."

Mom. My chest tightens and I tell myself to keep breathing. "I told you. I've been busy. I'm training for another race and have a bunch of bikes to fix up and sell."

He walks over to where I'm standing and puts a hand on my shoulder. "I know you're worried about Mom. If you need to talk about it, ask questions—"

"I'm fine." I know I say it too fast, but I don't care. "I . . . uh . . . have to go." I step away from him. "Do you think Gavin will care if I borrow his car?"

I hear him let out a small sigh. "He probably wouldn't even notice since he'll probably still be asleep when you get back, but your car is fixed. I've been working on it. It's in the driveway." He points to my keys which are sitting on the table.

"Oh. Thanks."

"Be careful." He looks sad. And I know it's my fault.

The sky is cloudy today. Perfect for a quick ride.

The air is crisp, cool even, as I pedal up the rocky terrain.

The uphill on this trail is kind of tough, I'll admit, but once I turn around at the top, going back down is my favorite part of the ride.

Sweat beads on my forehead as I switch gears again at the steepest part of the trail. My legs burn, my butt is numb, and I'm sweating from every possible place I can think of. Like a good biker should be.

It feels amazing.

It's one thing to bike for exercise and to . . . you know, stay in shape. It's a whole other thing to bike for the thrill. The challenge. The passion. Someday I'll get that sponsorship. Someday I'll maybe even do this for a living. I would love every second of it.

I ride for a while, enjoying the wind in my face and the adrenaline pumping. When I reach one of the hills, for some reason my bike feels heavier as I pedal my way to the top. It shouldn't feel that way since I'm in the lowest gear. I frown. It can only mean one thing. Once I finish my climb, I glance down at my tires and groan.

My front tire is deflating. Fast. So much for my perfect ride today.

I get off my bike and walk it a little ways until I reach my spot. I lean it against a tree while I take a look around. I need a moment to myself and then I'll change the tube and head home. I always carry a spare tube or two.

I'll never get over how beautiful it is up here. The birds singing, the trees blowing in the breeze. So peaceful.

I climb up on the rock Kelsie and I usually share and sit, wrapping my arms around my knees and pulling them to my chest as I stare out into the valley. The sun is up now and I'm glad I'm wearing sunglasses.

My helmet is bugging me, so I unhook it and take it off. My hair is a rat's nest I'm sure, but I slide it out of my elastic anyway, run my fingers through it, and shake my head. Letting it all loose feels good.

I enjoy the quiet. This is somewhere I can come to think. Where no one will bother me. I suck in a deep breath of nice clean air, smell the hint of rain. A few clouds inch their way overhead, and I kind of hope it sprinkles a little. It would cool me off at least. I frown as I hear someone coming up the trail.

So much for being alone up here.

The sound of wheels moving over rocks and dirt comes from my left. I glance over and recognize the black and red helmet at once.

Cole.

He slides his bike to a stop, looks over at me, and of course gets off his bike. "Marty? What are you doing up here all alone?"

I shrug. "Same as you I think." He glances around before leaning his bike against a tree. "Are you following me? I've seen you every day this week so far. That's not normal."

"I've just been lucky running into you." He smiles and, before I know it, he's climbing up on the rock next to me. "This is nice. Do you mind if I sit with you for a bit?"

"Sure." It's not like he's giving me a choice anyway. "Why are you up here today? I don't see you on this trail very often. You're usually on the more challenging ones."

"I didn't feel like going to my usual trail, but I wanted to get some practice in before Back Country. I need to be in top-notch shape to beat the other guys."

I roll my eyes. "Like you need practice."

"So, you admit I'm awesome." He nudges my shoulder and my face heats.

After I pull myself together, I look at him. "I didn't say that." I stare out into the valley again, trying to hide my smile.

"You totally think it."

I don't answer.

We're quiet as we both look at the view.

Cole's knee brushes mine and I glance over at him before scooting away. Not far, but enough. It doesn't stop the shiver his touch brings, though. Which is annoying. I don't like him. I'll never like him like that.

My body is kind of telling me something else, though. And the fact that I can't stop looking at him contradicts everything I'm trying to tell myself. It's weird that we're even sitting here together. Weird that I'm actually staying where I am and not back on my bike already. Weird that it's happened two days in a row. Weird that I kind of want to talk to him again.

"Have you forgiven me for arguing with you last night?"

I chuckle. "We didn't argue that much. And I'm not one to hold grudges."

He raises an eyebrow. "From the way you've avoided me for the last year, I thought otherwise."

"Biking grudges are different, so they don't count."

"Ah. I see. Thank you for clearing that up for me."

"You're welcome. Besides. About last night . . ." I hesitate, not wanting to admit he was right. But he was. "What you said was true. I don't know you very well and I haven't given you a chance because of some stupid rumors. I'm sorry I assumed things about you."

He shrugs. "It's okay. Maybe I'll tell you a truth or two one of these days."

I smile. "Maybe I'll tell you one of mine, too."

He leans back on his hands and stretches out his legs. "If I could only be so lucky."

I don't miss the sarcasm in his voice, but to my surprise, I laugh. "Yep."

"Always so mysterious."

"Right." I want to trust him. Especially since he's been so nice to me when I've been kind of a jerk. Maybe I should stop arguing with him all the time. It's getting kind of exhausting, to be honest.

"Do you sit here a lot?" he asks as he unhooks his helmet. He doesn't take it off, just lets the chin strap dangle near his neck.

I nod. "This is my favorite spot. I love it up here."

"Me too. I come here a lot to sit. Not this exact spot, but you know what I mean. It's quiet. I like to escape the chaos of every day. Do something simple."

I glance at him. "Sitting is simple?"

"The simplest. When you start thinking, that's when everything gets complicated."

I stare at him. Sometimes the things he says surprise me. He's so different from the person I thought he was. The player or womanizer. He's nothing like that. He's so . . . dare I say it: poetic? No. That sounds stupid. Besides, I've never been one for poetry so I don't even know what I'm talking about.

"This is nice. You and me. Sitting here together. I'm kind of getting used to it. It's much nicer than arguing with you every time we hang out."

"I don't argue with you *every* time."

"Sure . . ." He draws it out and chuckles.

He has a nice laugh.

"It's getting hot out here. Sometimes I hate the summer."

"I know. Me too. I should probably get back before I get sun burned."

"Your cheeks are already a little pink." He reaches out as if to touch my cheek, making my heart beat like crazy, and then drops his hand and turns away from me.

I follow his lead as he jumps down from the rock. When it's my turn, he reaches up and grabs my hand, helping me drop to the ground. My hand tingles from his touch, even through my gloves. It catches me off guard and, as I start toward my bike, I trip and almost fall on my face. Instead, Cole grabs me around the waist.

"Uh . . ." I put my hands on his chest as he steadies me. I stare at my hands and, after a moment's hesitation, drop them to my sides.

"You okay?" He's still hanging on to me and I can't help but notice his hazel eyes are more blue today. Light and clear. Like the sky. And . . . he's staring at me, totally realizing I'm checking him out.

"Yes." I pull away from him, embarrassed. "Sorry. I'm usually not so clumsy."

"I have that effect on girls."

"You make them clumsy?"

"No. They seem to fall all over themselves to get my attention."

"Oh, please." I step around him and wander over to my bike. I kneel down and pull my tool kit out of the pouch hooked to the bottom of my seat.

"You have a flat?"

"Yep."

"Do you need a hand?"

"Nope. I fix bikes for a living. Well . . . sort of. Not really a living, but . . . you know. For extra money and . . ." I stop talking when I see his amused expression. "I know how to change a flat, okay?"

He raises his hands up in defense. "Right on. I was trying to be a gentleman, asking if the lady would like some help, but you look like you've got it covered."

I grin. "This lady can take care of herself today."

"Obviously."

I frown at him.

"What?"

He chuckles again and I ignore him.

I could change a flat tire in my sleep I've done it so much. I grab my little blue tire lever and pry the tire away from the rim. Once I get the tire off, I grab the tube and pull it out. It's completely flat, so I set it on the ground next to me and pull a new tube out of the pouch. I check the tire for nasty stickers, since I accidentally plowed through a weed patch, and find a mother of a beast stuck on the other side. It's a doozy. No wonder I got a flat. After pulling it out, I check for more, but don't find any.

The entire time I work, I can feel Cole staring at me, but I don't look up. He makes me too nervous.

"You're fast."

I shrug. "Not really." I pull out a CO_2 cartridge after I put the new tube back in the tire and put it back to the rim. The CO_2 fills the tube up with air in seconds.

Good little tricks to have. Especially during a race. Once I'm finished, I stand and wipe off my dusty clothes.

"Nothing like watching a girl change a tire."

I glance over and give Cole a strange look. "What?"

"You just don't see it very often. It was pretty hot."

I chuckle. "Right." I tuck a strand of hair behind my ear and freeze when Cole's fingers touch my cheek. He rubs his thumb along my cheekbone and I'm afraid to look up at him again.

"You had some dirt on your face."

"Oh?"

He chuckles. "Yes. But seriously. I could watch you work on bikes all day. And I promise, I'm not trying to be creepy . . ."

"That was totally creepy." Not really, but I have to say it so it sounds like I don't enjoy him looking at me. Or enjoy me looking at him. Or . . . I'm confusing myself.

I put my helmet back on and, as I go to climb on my bike, Cole surprises me by grabbing my hand.

I stare at our hands as he steps closer to me, making my stomach do all sorts of crazy flips. "Can I ask you something?"

"Sure." I'm glad my voice is steady right now because I'm kind of terrified by the way he's looking at me. So serious. And there's something else in his expression that I can't quite read. Which scares me even more.

"Go out with me."

My eyes widen. "What?"

"You heard me. Go out with me. On a real date."

"Cole—"

"Before you say no, hear me out." He's still hanging on to my hand. I like it. Too much. So much so that I want to tell the voice in my head warning me to run away to shut up. Which is so *not* like me. "I was serious last night about wanting to get to know you better. The real you. The one I saw last year before . . . things happened."

Before Lucas happened. "I'm not the same—"

"I know. But I still like hanging out with you. I think you're an awesome biker, you're funny and sarcastic. A little stubborn sometimes, but it's cute on you."

"How can stubbornness be cute on me? It's not a piece of clothing."

He shrugs. "It doesn't make sense to me either, but the fact is you *are* stubborn."

"Okay. We all know that. Everyone knows that. Let's not bring it up anymore, okay?"

"Deal."

"Great."

"Anyway, back to asking you out. Like I said before. I like you." His gaze slides to the trees and he clears his throat before looking back at me. His cheeks are a little red. I've never seen him get embarrassed or uncomfortable before. To be honest, it's kind of cute. "And . . . I totally just embarrassed myself for saying that, but when it's true, it's true."

What the what? My face heats and I try to pull my hand away, but he doesn't let go. "I think you're . . . on something."

"Trust me. You'd know if I was on something." He laughs. "So, here's the deal. All I ask is one date. Put our differences aside and go to dinner."

"You sound like you're in a movie or something."

He laughs. "That's what I'm going for. Don't you like romantic comedies?"

"Some."

"Good. Because I swear I'm in one right now making a fool of myself."

I can't help it. I bust up laughing.

He chuckles as well as his cheeks turn pink. "Anyway, if the date sucks then you don't ever have to talk to me again. Unless you beat Whitney next Saturday. Then you'll have to join our team again. But I won't bug you about going out with me again."

"You won't?"

"No."

I study him. He's totally serious. I don't want to rush into saying yes, though. It would overinflate his ego even more. "I'll think about it."

"Really?"

"Yes."

"So, it's not a flat out no then?"

I shake my head. "No. I'll think about it and let you know."

"Great. Let's say Friday night."

"I haven't said yes yet!"

He grins. "You didn't say no either." He drops my hand and gets on his bike.

Flustered, I get on my bike too and wait to see what he's going to do. He lifts a hand and gestures toward the trail. "Ladies first."

I shrug. "Okay." I push off, and in seconds I'm flying downhill, guiding my bike over rocks and a tree root here and there. The wind blasts across my face, warmer than earlier. I know I'm going to be bright red once I get home.

We make it to the bottom in record time, and of course Cole is right behind me. I sort of wish he would have gone first so I could check out his moves. I know he's an awesome climber, but I've heard his downhill is even better.

"Need a ride home?" he asks as he takes his gloves off.

"I've got my car. Thanks, though."

He glances at the car and raises an eyebrow. "Glad it's working again."

"Me too."

I hook up my bike to my rack as he does the same to his. Once it's good and tight, I take my helmet and CamelBak off and throw them in the back seat.

Cole's watching me and I blush under his gaze. "This was nice, Marty. We should do it more often."

"Sure."

He grins and takes a step closer, leaning on my car door. "I guess I'll see you later."

"Okay."

"Have a good day, Marty."

I groan. "Do you really have to call me that every time you talk to me?"

He moves away from me and opens the door of his truck. "You love it."

I don't want to admit it's growing on me. A little.

CHAPTER 13

Friday comes fast. Too fast. I'm not ready for our date, and Cole is supposed to pick me up at seven.

Ten minutes from now.

I'm sure he'll be late. Aren't most guys? Honestly I have no idea. I haven't been out with someone for so long. I've kind of forgotten the proper etiquette and all that. That is, if the guy has any etiquette to begin with.

"Emmy, are you sure you don't want any dinner?" Dad yells from upstairs.

"Yes!" I yell while brushing my teeth. Toothpaste flies out of my mouth and onto the mirror in front of me.

Awesome.

My phone beeps and I frown at the text from Kelsie. She's wondering what I'm doing tonight. I send her a quick text that I'll call her a little later and shove the phone in my purse. If she knew I was going out with Cole, I'd never hear the end of it. And I can only deal with so much right now.

I hear someone coming down the stairs and jump as Mom comes and stands in the doorway with her arms folded. "So who's this mystery boy who's been taking up all of your time lately?"

"Cole." I spit my toothpaste out, rinse, and wipe off the mirror with a towel. "And he hasn't been taking up all my time. Not really." I stare at myself in the mirror, noticing the dark circles under my eyes. I haven't slept well this week. My outfit is cute at least. My favorite jeans and a new blue top. I'm not one for fashion, and Kelsie may not approve, but at least *I* like it.

"Who is he?"

I glance at Mom's reflection in the mirror and run my fingers through my hair. She looks tired. Almost as tired as me and, once again, the guilt takes over. "A . . . biking friend."

"Where are you going?"

"To dinner."

"A date?"

I pause. "Kind of. I think."

She smiles. "You haven't been on a date since—"

I don't want her to bring up Lucas, so I hurry and cut her off.

"I know."

"Well, I'm glad you're going out." She hesitates and touches my shoulder. "I was wondering if you're doing okay. After we talked on Sunday, you've been . . . distant."

"I'm fine." I step away. I should ask her how she's doing, but I don't. I don't want to know if she's losing her mind more than before. I don't want to know if she doesn't remember some of what I was like as a child. I want everything to go back to normal. It's easier to pretend like nothing's wrong, even though I'm not good at pretending.

The doorbell rings and I glance at the clock on my wall.

Great. He's early.

"Sounds like he's here," Mom says, glancing upstairs. "Please be back by a decent hour."

"I will. I'll . . . uh . . . see you when I get home." I want to hug her, maybe even kiss her cheek and tell her I love her, but I step around her instead.

I'm a coward.

"Be safe," she says, only loud enough for me to hear.

I race upstairs to open the door, and I'm surprised to see Gavin has beat me there instead. They're chatting like they're old friends or something. Weird.

Cole looks over as I come down the hall. His mouth drops open as he looks me over. I feel my cheeks heat, as usual, and tuck my hair behind my ear. "You look . . ." He clears his throat. "Good. You look good."

"Thanks." I don't know if I should tell him he looks good too or not. I decide against it. I'll probably embarrass myself somehow anyway. And besides, I'm sure he knows he looks good. Because he does. He really does. I shake that thought out of my head and grab my jacket. "You're early."

He shrugs. "Didn't want to be late. You ready to go?"

"Yep."

He opens the door. "Shall we?" He gestures outside and before I can move, Gavin steps in front of me.

"Have fun tonight." He turns toward Cole. "And don't even think about putting any moves on my little sister."

As if my face wasn't red enough already . . . "Gavin," I growl. Seriously. I'll kill him.

Cole laughs. "No worries. Your sister would probably punch me in the face if I tried anything anyway."

"Good to know I've taught her well," Gavin says, smiling at me. He glances at Cole again. "But seriously. I have eyes everywhere."

"Gavin," I snap. "Goodbye."

He grins and heads into the kitchen, leaving us alone and awkward by the door.

"He seems nice," Cole says.

I glare down the hall. "You'd think that, wouldn't you?" I sigh and walk out the door. Cole follows me.

Before I can open the door to his truck, he slides past me and opens it for me. "Allow me."

I roll my eyes but say thank you anyway. Even if he confuses the heck out of me, I'm glad he's a gentleman.

As I wait for him to walk around and get in, I smile at the song on the radio. I turn it up, just enough that we won't have to talk on the way to wherever we're going.

Cole gets in and the first thing he does is turn the radio down.

Perfect. Plan ruined.

"You really do look nice," he says. "Blue looks good on you. It matches your eyes."

My lips twitch. "Do you tell that to all your dates?"

He laughs. "Trust me when I say I don't go out much."

I turn to look at him. "Really?"

"Don't act so surprised." He glances over with a little grin on his face.

"I'm not acting. I just . . . don't really know what to think." From how he acts around girls, I could have sworn he took a different one out every night.

"Told you. Rumors." He shoots me a grin. "By the way, do you like Mexican food?"

My stomach growls. Yes. Of course I do, but sometimes too many beans can do a number on a person. Especially a stressed person. And yes. Even girls. "Yes. Mexican is fine."

He raises an eyebrow. "Fine as in . . . you like it? Or fine as in, 'eh, it's okay I guess.'"

I laugh. "I like it." My stomach growls again and I have a feeling I'm going to have a problem if we do decide on Mexican. I'll have to order something not so . . . beanie.

"Cool. We're not having Mexican food, though. Is In-N-Out okay?"

I snap to attention and gape at him. "Are you kidding? I love that place." Since they built one down the street from us, I can't get enough of it.

"It's the fries, huh?"

"The fries, the burgers. All of it." I find myself smiling and make sure my mouth is closed so I don't start drooling or something. I wouldn't put it past me . . .

"Awesome. The way to a girl's heart is through her stomach."

I have to agree with that. "Mine is. I love food."

He laughs. "My kind of girl then."

"Trust me. I'm not your kind of girl." Guys like girls who pick at their food, don't they? Ice cube eating girls. Skinny and tiny girls. Not . . . girls like me. I might be on the skinny side, but curves are my good friends.

"You'd be surprised what kind of girl I like."

I don't know what to say to that, so I wait for him to park and hum along to the song on the radio.

Dinner is heavenly. The burger, juicy and perfect with lots and lots of lettuce and yummy sauce. The fries? Delish. And a big fat glass of ice water to wash it all down.

"Seriously? Water?"

I shrug as I set my drink down. "Nothing like a tall glass of H2O to cool down."

He takes a swig of his Dr Pepper. "Water is okay, but only during a race. Other than that it's not my first choice. Or second. Or third even."

"It's the healthy choice."

"It's the plain choice."

"Like your choice is better." I gesture toward his Dr Pepper and wrinkle my nose. "It tastes like medicine."

"The best kind of medicine."

"Uh . . . no." I chuckle and finish off my fries.

"So. Good choice for a date?"

I smile. "You did good. I really wasn't looking forward to a date in a stuffy nice restaurant. You obviously know how I roll."

"I try to pay attention."

"Really?" I doubt he's ever seen me come here. If he has, it was either a coincidence or he was stalking me. I'm doubting anyone would ever go to the lengths to stalk me. I mean, come on. It's me. "I don't think I've ever told you I like this place. How did you know?"

He leans forward and whispers, "I asked Kelsie what your favorite place to eat was."

"Ah. Research with the best friend then."

He folds his arms and leans back against the booth. "Of course."

"Impressive. You can get a lot out of her. Unfortunately." Hopefully he didn't ask her about anything embarrassing.

"I try." He leans forward again, resting his arms on the table. "Seeing how this date is going well, we should do this more often."

I don't say anything, just sip my water.

"No answer? Obviously I'm failing at something or you would have agreed with me."

"Cole . . ."

He raises a hand. "It's okay. I'll try harder." He piles our wrappers on the tray and leans back against the booth. "So . . . what do you like to do? Besides biking, of course."

I twirl my ice around with my straw and shrug. "I don't know. I guess I like to listen to music. I like to read, fix bikes, but most of my free time is spent on the mountain."

"Nice."

"What about you?" For some reason, I've never thought about what else he does. I've never wanted to know, but now I'm curious.

"I like to long board a little. And play the guitar."

My eyes widen. "You play the guitar? My friend Oakley plays the guitar. Or played, I guess." Before Lucas died, she played all the time. I loved listening to her play. I always wanted her to teach me.

He gives me a funny look. "Yep. Started when I was six."

"You're good then."

"Eh. Depends on who you ask."

"Do you have a band or anything?"

He snorts. "No."

"Why not? If you're that good, why don't you play for people?"

"I don't want to show off."

Something about the way he won't meet my eyes makes me wonder if he's really telling the truth. "Would you play for me sometime?"

"Maybe. If you're nice to me."

"I'm totally nice."

"Sometimes." He winks and I pretend to throw my water at him.

"Fair enough." I twirl my ice around in my cup again. I don't want to talk about me. Especially the parts of me I don't like. Like my meanness. Sometimes it just comes out when I don't want it to. I try a different tactic to change the subject. "Since I'm actually out on a date with you and didn't turn you down . . . I think I deserve to know a truth."

"Ah. Should have seen that one coming."

"I like to catch people off guard."

"This is true." He taps his fingers on the table and looks like he's thinking of something to tell me. "I broke my arm snowboarding once."

"Really?"

"Really. First time I went with a bunch of friends. I thought I was cool and wanted to show off, so I did a front flip off a jump and the next thing I knew, I was getting helped down the mountain by the ski patrol."

I can't help it. I'm laughing.

He puts a hand to his chest like he's offended. "It was traumatizing."

"And kind of hilarious. I can just see you showing off in front of everyone."

"I haven't been since."

"How old were you?"

"Thirteen." He frowns for a second like it was a horrible memory and smiles again.

"Didn't you grow up in California?"

"We moved a lot."

"Oh."

He smiles again. "Your turn."

"Ah. My turn." I rub my hands together. "Just one truth?"

"Yep. Anything you want. Preferably something not everyone knows."

"Fine." I wrack my brain for something personal, but not too revealing. "I don't date a lot."

He gives me a look. "Whatever. I don't believe it."

"Really. I'm serious."

"So . . . you don't date. Does that mean you've never kissed anyone then?"

My cheeks heat. Did he really have to go and ask *that* question? "I never said that. I said I don't date. That doesn't have anything to do with kissing."

"Interesting. So you play the field but don't settle down. I get it." I should be offended, but he's smiling and I know he's joking. At least . . . I think he is.

"I had a wild couple of years. What can I say?" I laugh because it's not even remotely true. Sure I kissed a few guys here and there, but there was only one person I ever really wanted to kiss and never got the chance. The only guy I've ever loved. Lucas. And thinking about him makes me sad. The only person I ever told was Mom. I told her everything the day Lucas told me his cancer was back. Everything. And Kelsie knows now, but back then? No one else. Sure, people knew we were friends, like my dad and brother and his family, but my feelings for him were secret. Just like he kept the fact that he loved me secret.

Too many secrets.

I don't want to go through that ever again. It's one of the reasons I never get close to anyone anymore. Besides Kelsie, of course. Because after all is said and done, I'm always left alone. Now more than ever. Even Mom will forget me sooner or later.

"I don't picture you as a wild girl."

I frown, snapping back into the conversation. "I'm not."

He's thoughtful for a moment. "I thought you dated that Lucas kid."

I freeze. "No."

"Really? The way you react when I mention his name makes me think there was more than just friendship going on."

"I really don't want to talk about this right now."

"Sorry. It's just . . . sometimes talking about things make you feel better."

"Trust me. Talking about Lucas won't make me feel better."

"Fair enough."

"Thanks," I whisper, grateful he's not pushing the subject.

"You ready to head out?"

"Yep."

"Sorry it's kind of a short date. I thought you'd want to be rid of me pretty quick."

I chuckle. "I'm not that rude."

"I think you just admitted you enjoy my company."

"Surprisingly, it's not that bad." I stare at my hands and can't stop the smile that creeps to my lips.

I have to admit, I'm kind of enjoying hanging out with him. He keeps things interesting. And as much as I miss Lucas, it's nice to have someone kind of like him to talk to again. Someone who likes to spend time with me, for me. Someone who treats me well and actually wants to get to know me. Someone who knows how to tease. And Cole totally has that one down.

"Perfect. Just the reaction I was looking for."

I glance up as he stands, and I can't explain the warmth that rushes through my body when he smiles at me.

I'm in big trouble.

CHAPTER 14

The drive home is quieter than before. Cole focuses on the road, and I focus on the houses passing by the window. Perfect houses with white picket fences and wrap-around porches. Green well-kept yards, fancy mailboxes, and big trees shading the lawns.

A neighborhood out of a movie. I could live here when I'm older. With kids running around the yard while my husband and I watch them from the porch. I can be happy. Everyone deserves to be happy, right? Even when you feel like your life is crumbling down and you keep getting one piece of bad news after another. There's a tiny chance for happiness after all is said and done.

Right?

As I contemplate my emotions swimming around, I glance at Cole again and try to analyze our date. Part of me wants to shut him out and pretend like what I'm feeling when he's around isn't real. The other part wants to get to know him better. To go out with him again. To keep talking.

The music plays softly on the radio as he drives. The silence isn't awkward at all, just different. Like something's changed. I haven't decided if it's a good thing or a bad thing.

He pulls into my driveway a few minutes later and turns the truck off. With a small smile, he jumps out and comes around to open my door. Once I'm out, he walks me to the porch, his hand at his sides, all friend like. I wonder if he'll try to make a move. I'm guessing no, since this was kind of a test date, but I don't seem to know what he's ever really thinking, so he could surprise me.

If he does make a move, though . . . I don't know what I'll do.

We reach the bottom of the porch and he stops and turns toward me. "So this was fun."

"It was."

"We should do it again."

I nod, but don't say anything. Once I make it up the three steps to the porch, I stop and turn toward him, waiting for . . . I'm not sure what.

He puts his hands in his pockets and watches me. "I have a question."

"Okay?"

"You know I like you. I've told you as much. So, the question of the day is . . . do I have a chance at all?"

My heart quickens, and I back up a step. "Cole . . . I . . ."

Does he? Could I let someone like him in? The answer is . . . I don't know. I really don't know.

"Really." He takes a step closer. "I need to know now if it will ever go anywhere. I know the biking thing is a big deal for you. The captain thing is a big deal. I know you need to prove something by beating Whitney or whatever next Saturday, but after all that's over, I'd like to take you out again. If . . . you know. If you don't mind."

I could break his heart. I could tell him to leave me alone right now and be done with it. Ignore him on the trails and in school next fall. Never look back so I'll never get hurt. But something stops me. So instead of pushing him away, all I do is smile. "After I beat Whitney, we can talk more."

He frowns. "About that. Do you need any help? I could go riding with you. Give you some pointers. You only have a week to train and I could help you a bit."

My eyes narrow. "Why? Are you so sure Whitney's gonna win?" It comes out short, even though I don't mean it to.

"No, I have to . . ." He trails off and looks at the ground. "Look. I was going to tell you this earlier, but I didn't know how." He pulls something out of his jacket pocket and hands it to me.

Biking gloves.

"What are these for?" The wheels in my head start turning. These gloves are nice. Like top-of-the-line nice. I'd never spend so much on a pair of gloves like these.

I glance up at him and he hesitates before speaking. "A few weeks ago, Edge approached Whitney and me."

I don't hear anything else. All I can do is stare at the gloves and try to control my scattered emotions. "You're sponsored? Both of you?"

He rocks back and forth and finally settles, his eyes meeting mine. "Yes."

I nod and bite my tongue. *Don't freak out. Don't freak out.* I knew it was coming, since he's amazing, but why did he wait so long to tell me? Especially about Whitney? "Congratulations."

"Like I said before. I was gonna tell you earlier, but didn't know how." He's trying to read the look on my face. I can see it in his eyes. Trying to figure out how much to tell me. If I'm angry. If I'm upset.

I think of Mom and Dad keeping Mom's diagnosis from me. And now Cole and Whitney are sponsored? Does no one in this world trust me? I don't get it. I don't understand. What's with all the secrets? Are they trying to make me go crazy?

"You got this a few weeks ago?"

"Yes."

My temper rises, just a tad. "Huh. So, I basically made an idiot out of myself when I asked Whitney for a rematch. And you just stood there and let me."

His eyes widen. "Why would that make you an idiot? Whitney's good, but she knows you're good, too. She sees you as a threat. Beating you one-on-one will actually be a challenge for her."

I'm not a challenge. I don't have a sponsor. I don't have people watching me and begging me to race for them. I'm just . . . me. I put the gloves back in his hands feeling . . . sad, of all things. Which is weird. I thought I was going to be angrier. But now I'm confused. Confused and hurt by everyone.

I look up at him and note the strange emotions on his face. What is he trying to prove by telling me this? I turn and struggle trying to get my keys out of my pocket to open the stupid door. I need to get away from him. I need to get to the safety and sanctuary of my room. Away from everyone. "Goodnight."

"Come on, Emmy. This is not how I wanted to end our date."

I let out an annoyed breath. "It wasn't even a date. You took me out to be nice. That's all. So I wouldn't feel like such a loser when Whitney beats me again."

"Stop." He grabs my arm, stopping me as I try to get my key in the lock. "What is it with you? Why are you so against me? I'm trying here. I've been trying for a year and when I finally make some progress with you, you start . . . I don't know. Feeling all sorry for yourself."

"What do you want me to do, Cole? Do you want me to worship you or something? Tell you how good you are? Beg you for your help because I can't handle things on my own?"

"No. You know me better than that."

"Do I? Are we even friends? Because the last time I checked, we weren't."

He steps closer. My heart hammers in my chest as his hazel eyes search mine. "I don't know. Are we?"

My eyes narrow and I'm so close to pushing him off the porch I can feel it. "You—"

He grabs my hands as I try to shove him away and instead of him flying backward, he pulls me close so I'm inches away from his face. "Nice try." He looks amused. Not mad at all. "If you would have let me finish, I would have told you something else. I'm bringing my sponsor to your race against Whitney. To watch you. As in, if they like you, they'll sponsor you, too."

It takes a second to register. "Are you serious?"

"Of course I'm serious. If you'd stop thinking of me as the bad guy, you might actually trust me a little."

I stare at him. He's a little frustrated with me; I can see it. But there's something else there, too. "I . . ." No words. No words will form, so I continue to stare. My eyes flick to his lips as his move to mine.

So close. So close. He's so very close. His breath on my skin makes me shiver, and as much as I want to slap him, another part of me wants him to kiss me.

Something's seriously wrong with me.

"Cole . . . I . . ." Too close now. Too close. I lean away, just a little, and so does he.

He stares at me, lines creasing his brow as a frown forms on his lips. "I'm sorry," he breathes. "I shouldn't have . . ." He trails off.

I'm not sure if he's talking about the sponsor or something else. Instead of asking, I step away. Disappointment washes over me as he drops my hands. "Thank you for dinner." I turn away, trying to forget the way he's looking at me but the thought makes me turn back around. "I'll see you tomorrow."

"I'm glad to hear it," he says with a small smile. "Until next time."

I go inside and shut the door. I'm surprised Mom and Dad aren't hovering anywhere close—especially Dad, to make sure I'm not making out on the front porch or something. Instead of finding them, I go down to my room. As I lay on my bed, my head is a sea of strange and unfamiliar emotions that I can't quite figure out.

It's going to be a long night.

CHAPTER 15

Over the next week, all I do is train. After Cole told me he was sponsored, I made a goal to do everything I could to beat Whitney. And to show him I'm good enough to beat her without his "training."

I train so hard, I can't catch my breath.

Push myself harder than I've ever pushed.

Every day, I wake up at six in the morning and go up to the trails to ride for an hour or two, then go home, shower, do another set of workouts to keep my stamina up, and pretty much stay in my room and strategize the rest of the time.

I don't see Cole. He texts me to see what I'm doing a few times, but I tell him I'm busy. I can't worry about him when I'm supposed to be focusing on my race.

Kelsie rides with me a few times, but she knows how serious I am about this race so she lets me do my own thing. She knows when I'm in the zone and leaves me alone.

I ignore my family. They know it. I know it. I feel bad about it, but this race means everything to me.

I want to win. I want to beat Whitney. Not just beat her to rub it in her face, either. I want to do it for me. And the more I train, the more obsessed I become.

After an especially hot day, I plow through my bedroom door, throw my biking crap in the corner, and flop onto my bed. My body hurts, and I'm sunburned and exhausted.

Someone knocks on my door then and I jump, my eyes flying open. I must have fallen asleep.

"Come in," I croak and clear my throat.

Mom opens the door and comes inside. "Hey. How's it going?" she asks.

"Good. Sorry, really tired today." I rub my eyes and sit up, noting how gross I smell since I'm still in my biking clothes.

"Judging from your clothes, you went biking again?"

"Yeah."

"Is there a day I can come watch you?"

"You can't really watch, Mom. You have to be on a bike yourself."

"Maybe you could take me sometime."

I shrug. "Maybe."

She sighs. "I know you've been avoiding me, honey. I'm sorry I've made you so upset, I just . . . I didn't know what to do." She meets my eyes. "So, our girls' night is next week. What do you want to do?"

I shrug. "I don't care."

"Well, do you *want* to go do something? We could see that chick flick you wanted to see or get a pedicure or something."

I shake my head. "I've got a lot of stuff going on next week. Maybe we can rain check?"

She hesitates before nodding. "Sure." She gets up and makes her way across the room. "You know I'm still the same person, right? I haven't changed, honey. You don't need to be afraid to spend time with me."

I nod and swallow the lump in my throat.

"Don't stay in here all day. I'll make something for lunch, okay? So come upstairs in about ten minutes. It will be on the table."

"Okay."

She closes the door and I lay back on my bed.

Guilt for being so distant gnaws at me. But as usual, I do nothing about it.

CHAPTER 16

Race day. It's early. The sun hasn't come up yet, but of course I'm wide awake. I turn over on my side and glance at the clock. Six in the morning. I don't have to be at the trail for three hours.

Curse my early rising genes.

I hear someone walking around upstairs, but I stay in bed, not wanting to have a conversation with anyone this early. The person walks in the bathroom and the door shuts right before the shower turns on. Dad, I'm sure. The early riser I take after.

I pull out my phone and look at my email and a text from Kelsie. Nothing important. Instead of turning it off, a thought pops into my head. Mom. Her disease. After a second, I do something I should have done a long time ago: I type in "early Alzheimer's disease."

My finger hovers over the search button and I take a deep breath before pushing it.

A bunch of links pop up and I scan through them before clicking on one.

Early-onset Alzheimer's Disease. Or Familial Alzheimer's Disease. The correct term used for cases diagnosed before age sixty-five.

I frown as I scroll through the symptoms, recognizing a few Mom has experienced, now that I think about it.

Some symptoms of Alzheimer's can be memory loss, challenges in problem solving, difficulty performing tasks, confusion, trouble speaking, misplacing things and forgetfulness, withdrawal from social events, mood swings. As the disease progresses, I read, the patient may not be able to care for his or herself and must be under twenty-four-hour care to avoid harm to self or accidents.

I look through the article. Words jump out at me as I read and I start to feel sick to my stomach.

Devastating effects on careers. Hard for family members to deal with. Young children suffer from parent not being able to care for them anymore.

Family suffers.

Hard for family.

Devastating for spouses and family.

Memory loss.

I turn my phone off and throw it toward the end of my bed before I lean back and stare at the ceiling.

I need to talk to someone.

And the only someone I feel comfortable talking to besides my parents is in this house.

I push the covers off my bed and head upstairs. I know Gavin is asleep, but I don't care. I sneak into his room and close the door behind me.

He doesn't even move.

"Gav," I say as I sit on the edge of his bed.

He groans softly, but doesn't move.

134

"Gav." I touch his bare shoulder and he shrugs it off and puts his pillow over his head.

"Gavin."

He sighs and sits up after a few seconds.

I cover my eyes as he makes sure his blanket is wrapped around him. "Do you really have to sleep in your underwear?"

"Yes." He rubs his hand over his face and looks up at me. "What are you doing in here? Haven't you met your quota for waking me up early this month?" His voice is annoyed, but then he gets a good look at me and frowns. "You okay?"

I take a deep breath. "Not really."

"What's wrong?"

I shrug. "Just worried about Mom."

He's quiet for a moment. "Me too. Did you talk to her or something?"

"No. I don't even know what to say to her. I'm not meaning to avoid her, it's just . . ."

"Hard. I know. I've been avoiding her, too."

"I looked up Alzheimer's on the Internet. It's . . . awful. What's going to happen to her is not going to be good. I can't . . . I can't even think about it. It makes my heart hurt. It makes me want to cry."

"Don't cry."

I want to, but I hold it in for his sake. "I won't. I'm just . . . scared."

"Don't be scared, Em."

Emotion builds under the surface, and I fight to keep myself under control. "What do we do?"

He shrugs. "We stick together. Act like everything's fine, I guess. At least until we get used to it. I'm not sure what else we're supposed to do. Everything's not fine, obviously, but . . . I don't want to be all depressed all the time. You know? And Mom's still Mom. We need to be there for her. We need to make her feel like we're with her, not against her. Make her feel she's not alone. And Dad, too."

"Yeah. I know." I stare at the floor, wondering how he can even pretend everything's normal and fine.

"Hey." He reaches out and grabs my hand. "It's gonna be okay."

"How do you know?"

"I'm your big brother. I know everything."

Instead of rolling my eyes, I wrap my arm around his neck and give him a hug. "Thanks for being my big brother."

"Didn't really have a choice . . ."

I smack him in the shoulder and jump away as he tries to retaliate. "Nice try."

"You're pretty spry in the morning."

"I just have cooler moves than you." I touch the doorknob. "You can go back to sleep now."

He pauses. "Hey. Do you want to watch a movie or something later? I don't have to work."

"Sure. That sounds great."

"I'm picking."

"Of course." I smile and turn to leave.

"Em." The softness of his voice makes me turn to face him again. "If you need to talk, vent, whatever. I'm here."

I smile back at him. "I know."

CHAPTER 17

A few hours later, I'm getting ready for my race. *The race.* Me against my sponsored nemesis. I wonder if she knows I know.

She's so going down.

I stare at my reflection in the mirror. I slide my hair back in an elastic, put a bit of mascara on so Kelsie doesn't kill me, and head down the hallway.

"Where are you off to this morning?"

Mom sits on the couch, a book in her hand. I'm taken aback for a second; I don't remember the last time I saw her read a book.

"Oh. Uh . . . I'm going riding."

"Why?"

I sigh. "Because it's fun? And I have nothing better to do today."

"You could stay home and chat with me. We could go to lunch or a movie or—"

"No, no, that's okay. Maybe another day." I give her half a smile and she looks back at me as disappointment flickers across her features. It takes her a second to recover. She sets her book on the couch next to her and her hands rest in her lap. "Where are you riding today?"

I debate on telling her the truth, and that I'm going to Park City, but I have a feeling she won't let me go. So . . . I improvise. "Ogden." Okay, improvise isn't really the right word. I lie. Enough to make her not question anything and to stop the conversation from delving into stuff I don't want to talk about. And maybe also because she lied to me for so long.

She sits up straighter. "It's not one of your races, is it? I'd really like to come to one."

"No." Technically it's not *that* kind of race.

"You're not going alone, are you?"

"No. Kelsie's going with me. And she's driving, if that makes you feel any better." My eyes flit to the door. I can't look at her. Lying to her feels . . . wrong. But I know she won't let me drive all the way to Park City just to spend money on the ski lift and ride down a hill on a bike.

"Don't be gone long. Please."

"Okay." Relieved the questions ended, I head toward the door.

"Emmy."

I stop and look over my shoulder. "Yeah?"

"I want to talk to you when you get home."

"About what?"

She gives me a pointed look. "You know what I'm talking about, Emmy. I've tried to talk to you several times and you just make excuses or leave the house. You've avoided me for two weeks now. I want to talk to you about my . . . condition. I want you to know that I'm okay. I'm going to be okay. I know you're worried and you're dealing with it the best you can right now, but you can't ignore it. Or me. I want to do our girls' nights again. We can't stop doing those. Okay?"

I close my eyes, trying to fight the headache coming on. "I'll . . . talk to you about it when I get home."

"Okay. Be careful."

"I will."

Kelsie's already in the driveway when I open the door. "Hey," she says, getting out of her car.

I hand her my bag of gear. "I'm ready, I just have to grab my bike."

"Okay."

After locking up my bike on her rack, we head toward Park City.

The drive is kind of different for us. We don't really talk. I don't bring up Cole. Or the date. Or the sponsorship. The weird feelings I get when I'm around him. I don't say anything about how nervous I am to see him today. Nothing.

Until, of course, Kelsie brings it up.

"So, have you talked to Cole since the infamous date?" Kelsie turns the radio down even though she's humming along with the song.

"That would be a no."

Instead of slamming on the brakes or something, she speeds up, almost plowing us into a mailbox.

"What? Why?"

"I don't know. I've just been busy, I guess."

The corner of her mouth twitches. "And?"

"And what?"

"You haven't tried to call him?"

"Nope."

"He hasn't called you?"

"He tried a few times."

"And you didn't answer because . . .?"

"I really don't like where this is going . . ."

"You like him. That's why." She glances at me and giggles.

I can't help it. I smile back at her, and pretty soon we're laughing our heads off.

"I knew this would happen. I was hoping it would. You two are meant for each other. Seriously."

"I don't know about that. We argue a lot."

"The best couples do. As long as they make up quick."

"Right." I stare out the window. "I'm just . . . scared."

"Because of Lucas, right?"

I shrug. "Part of it."

"It's okay to move on, Em. I know you loved him, but . . . he's gone. I mean, there will always be a part of him with you, of course, but it's good to move on. And seeing how interested Cole is? You should give him a chance."

I sigh. "I know. He probably thinks I hate him, though, since I haven't called him back. It's been a week." I twist my ring, thinking of what life would be like if Lucas were still here.

"It's only been a week. He's fine. He's a guy."

"What does that even mean?"

"I don't know."

I chuckle, still twisting my ring. "Do you remember when we went skiing with Lucas and Oakley sophomore year?"

She chuckles. "Yeah. You were horrible." She grins at me and I smile.

"I really was, wasn't I?"

"Obviously, since you've never gone again. Bright side, though? You got a lot of 'tips' from Lucas. He didn't leave your side the entire time we were on the mountain."

"I wonder if Oakley knew how much I . . ." I trail off and shake my head.

"She knew. We talked about you two once."

"What?"

She shrugs. "She hated his girlfriend, so we talked about it. She would have been fine if you two would have hooked up. One of her friends dating her brother? It might have been a little awkward sometimes, but she said she would have been cool. Because she liked you. She knew you'd treat him well."

"I never said anything because of her. I didn't want things to get weird."

"Things would have been fine." She sits there a moment, her eyes focused on the road. "I'm sorry he's gone, Em. Really."

"I miss him. I miss Oakley, too. She was never the same after he died. I hope she's doing okay in California. She's been gone almost six months now."

"I hope she'd doing okay, too. So, about Cole . . . you really ought to give him a chance, you know. He might help you. Move on, I mean."

I doubt that. "After our date . . . he told me he was sponsored. Whitney, too."

"Really?"

"Yeah." I turn back toward her. "You didn't know, did you?"

"No."

That makes me feel a little better. But I'm still mad he didn't tell me earlier. "I don't know what he's trying to do, Kels. I don't know how I feel about . . . everything."

I think of Lucas again. I don't know if I can ever love someone the way I loved him. And the funny thing is, we weren't ever together. We were just friends. He admitted he loved me a week before he died, which felt like it changed my life forever, but now he's gone. And Cole. Cole's a great guy. I never saw that before now. "I'm confused, Kels. I don't date. I can't do relationships. Even relationships that aren't *real*." I stare out the window again.

"You don't have to know right now. All you need to do is let it flow. Things happen naturally. If you like him, go with it. Don't just jump into it, though. Play a little hard to get for a bit. If you don't, I haven't taught you anything."

I chuckle as I think of all the hearts she's broken. "I will. I still don't know if I like him for sure."

She rolls her eyes. "Sure."

I'm quiet for a while, thinking of Cole, how I feel about him. Why I feel that way. What I'm going to do about it.

I have no idea.

"So. All boy talk aside. Are you ready to race today?"

"Yeah, I think so."

"You sure you don't want to skip the race and go shopping or something?"

I laugh. "Only you know how to ruin a girl's day."

"Totally not ruining material. Shopping is awesome." She sinks down in her seat. "Seriously."

"We can do it if you want. I'll call a forfeit with Whitney and we can hang out all day."

She laughs, knowing I'd never give up a chance at a race. "No. I want to see you kick Whitney's skinny butt. That's why we're going to Park City, right? But maybe we can go shopping at the outlets on the way back. Shopping makes any day better."

"I can't say I agree with the whole shopping thing, but I'll come with you for moral support. And I owe you a shopping day anyway."

"Best day ever."

I frown at the prospect of her lugging me around the outlets and making me try stuff on, especially after this race. Shopping is the absolute worst thing she could make me do today. Or any day really. "How are we even friends?" I ask.

She chuckles. "I have no idea."

CHAPTER 18

The breeze whispers against my skin, and I close my eyes, breathing in the fresh air. I haven't been to Deer Valley Ski Resort in forever. It's so . . . beautiful. So green with tons of trees. Even if it's a pain in the butt to drive here, it's worth it. It's such a cozy city. Cute houses and shops everywhere. People out walking dogs or jogging along the little streets.

I especially love it in the winter when the skiers are out and about. Holed up in hotels and hanging out in the lobby, or walking the streets with their trendy coats and scarves, holding mugs of hot cocoa on cold nights. It's like one of those Christmas movies on the Hallmark Channel with the quaint inns and fireplaces and love stories unfolding in front of our eyes.

Sigh. Call me a romantic. I don't care. I love it here.

"You ready for this?"

I look at Kelsie on the ski lift next to me. "Yes." I'm happy she's here with me. She makes me less nervous and gives me good vibes. And I need all the good vibes I can get today. After not talking to Cole since our date, and knowing that I'm going to see him soon, I'm all hot and bothered.

And I don't like it. At all.

"It looks pretty steep down there."

I glance over the rail. "I'll be fine."

"Promise me you won't go all crazy and hurt yourself trying to win."

I roll my eyes. "Kels. Don't worry. I got this."

"You sure?"

"Absolutely."

We get to the top of the mountain and get off the lift. I wait for my bike to come around on the next bench. The person working the lift stops it, and I unhook my bike and roll it off to the side toward the trail.

"Nice of you to join us, ladies. You look nice and ready, Marty. How are you feeling this fine morning?"

I cringe at Cole's voice and the way it makes my heart flutter, but turn around with a cocky smile. "I'm feeling fine, actually. Where's—"

"Emmy! You made it!" Whitney walks her bike over to us with a huge grin on her face. A few people from the high school biking team stand behind her, bikes and helmets at the ready. I wave at them, but on the inside I'm not super thrilled they're here. This was supposed to be between Whitney and me. I didn't want a huge audience.

Whitney stops when she reaches my side. "I wasn't sure you'd actually show, but now that you're here, let's get this over with."

"Bring it on, then."

She just smiles and shakes her head as she walks past me. Cole laughs, and I wait for him to say something sarcastic to go along with my attempt at sounding cool, but he doesn't. All he does is rub his hands together. "Let's get started." He walks over to his bike and puts on his helmet.

"What are you doing?" I ask.

"I'm coming down after you guys finish the race. You think I just came up here to watch?" He shakes his head. "Not a chance. This is one of my favorite trails."

"Oh. Uh . . . I'll see you at the bottom then." I try to look away, but I'm sort of distracted by the way the muscles in his arms flex as he puts his gloves on.

Kelsie grabs my arm. "I never thought I'd say this . . ."

"If you're about to compliment his spandex, I'll never go riding with you again."

"He has a nice butt. That's all I was going to say."

I shake my head and put my gloves on. "No one looks good in spandex, so stop checking out my . . . friend."

"Friend?" She looks like she's going to laugh, but she winks at me instead. "Also, FYI, I can check out whoever I want." She grins and hands me my helmet.

"True."

"And just so you know, he does look good in spandex. He has a nice butt. And I totally saw you checking him out earlier."

I roll my eyes, but deep down I have to agree.

She hands me my CamelBak, and I strap it on. "I was also going to tell you to be careful."

"I'll be fine. See you in a bit." I walk my bike over to where Whitney's waiting at the top of the trail.

"Ready?" she asks, adjusting her sunglasses.

"Yep."

Cole's on his phone but closes it when I look at him. I wonder if it's the sponsor he invited. And if he came, where is he? I'm suddenly a little more nervous than before. "You sure you're up to this, Marty? You've been on this trail before?"

I raise an eyebrow, wondering why he's making me look weak in front of Whitney. "Does it matter?" Actually, I hadn't been on this particular trail before. Which kind of makes me nervous, but I try my hardest not to show it.

He shakes his head. "No. But be careful. It's rockier than the trails you're used to. And slick in some places."

I brush him off. "Thanks for the warning." I turn back and look at the trees again. I can do this. I'm fine. There's nothing to worry about.

He grabs my arm. "Hey. Are you okay?"

"I'm good. Why?" I touch my face, suddenly self-conscious.

"I want to make sure you're not mad still. You haven't been answering my texts, so I figured you were. I'm sorry. I should have told you about the sponsor stuff earlier"

I sigh. "It's fine. Not gonna lie, I was a little surprised you threw it on me right before the race, but it's okay. I'm good now. I've been training every day so I can beat her. Which I can do, you know."

"I know. And just so *you* know, I had a really nice time with you on our date."

I turn to look at him, surprised at the sincerity on his face. "I did too." And I did.

"Then we're cool, right?"

Whitney steps between us. "Can you guys do whatever you're doing after the race? I've got a hair appointment in an hour, so let's do this."

He stares at me for a second and finally grins. "Okay. You ready?" He glances toward his friends, who look as anxious as I feel. Though, they're just anxious to get riding; I can tell they're sick of waiting for us to start. "Mark, you timing this?"

Mark nods and touches his watch. Cole glances at me. "Ready?"

I nod.

"I'll see you at the bottom, Emmy!" Kelsie yells. "Kick her butt!"

"I can't wait to see her try," Whitney says.

I grin at Cole, and he smiles back. "May the best biker win." He gestures to the trail.

Mark yells, "Go!"

I don't hesitate at all, just push off and hang on as my bike flies down the mountain. My adrenaline kicks in, and I smile as I make every turn. It's an amazing feeling. Like I'm really flying. Trees surround me, and it feels like I'm alone in a huge forest, feeling free and more alive than I've felt in weeks.

My bike soars over a rock and lands on a thin board a few yards away. I ride over it like I've done it a million times. The truth is though, I've never ridden a trail this complicated, but I'm holding my own and it's awesome.

I wonder if Whitney's right behind me, but don't turn around. I don't want to miss any part of this ride.

After riding for a few quiet minutes, the distractions start rolling in. Thoughts of Mom pop into my head. How hurt she looked when I left her on the couch this morning. How Dad has been bugging me to talk to them. Why am I being so weird about it? Mom's still here. She's still very much herself. I should be happy about that, right?

But then thoughts of what I read on the Internet hit me. Her not remembering my name someday hits me hard. I can't handle that. I can't see her struggling to put a name to her own daughter's face. And when I have my own kids, she won't even know who they are. I shake my head and get it out of my mind.

Not today. Don't think about it.

Focus on the race and that's it.

My thoughts change directions, and I frown at where they lead. To Whitney. How much I want to beat her. I don't know why I want it so bad. I just do. I want to be captain again. Crave it. Or maybe it's the fact that I'd give anything to do this for a living and want to prove it by winning this. By winning the Back Country race in a few weeks. I have to prove I'm as good as her. As good as Cole even. Good enough to get a sponsor. Good enough for him to . . . I don't know. Like me? Because honestly, I'm having a hard time talking myself out of liking *him*.

I'm guessing I'm about halfway down the mountain now. It's a little slick, but as long as I have control, I'll be fine.

Stay in control. You've got this. The words keep repeating through my head, and I use them to keep moving. Keep pedaling. Keep myself together. Victory is at my fingertips. I can almost taste it. The wind rushes by and my adrenaline pumps through my veins, making me push harder. I swear I've never gone so fast in my life.

I wish Lucas were here to see me ride. He'd be cheering me on at the bottom. He loved coming to my races.

A hill is ahead, and I shift gears right as I start the climb. As far as I know, I'm still alone. But as I start up the hill, sweating and panting, Whitney rides by me like it's nothing. She doesn't say anything, which makes me feel a little better. No cockiness or smart remarks. Just her and her game face. But seeing how easy she passed me makes me realize she's going to beat me no matter how hard I ride.

I keep pushing myself and reach the top, right after she does. I switch gears again and head down the rocky terrain, bumping up and down on my seat. My tires slide a little and as I careen out of control, I pull on both my brakes.

Which is the stupidest thing I could do.

Everything goes in slow motion as I flip over my handle bars. I land hard on my back, try to twist onto my side to catch myself, but start rolling down the mountain instead. Fire tears through my forehead and pain radiates through my body each time I hit a sharp rock.

I'm well aware of the sound of my bike crashing down the mountain after me. When I finally roll to a stop, it flies over me, almost hitting me in the face. I hear it land in some bushes a few feet away.

It takes me a minute to realize what happened as I try and catch my breath.

Everything's quiet. I'm floating. It feels like I'm not connected to my body anymore, but I know I am because I'm still awake and staring up into the trees above me.

My head is swimming. I close my eyes and open them again. Trees. And black dots.

Blink.

More trees. More dots.

Pain.

The only thing I hear is my shallow, noisy breathing.

I lay on the ground for a while, trying to make the dizziness go away.

After letting the crash sink in, cursing a few times and trying not to cry, I force myself to sit up, my body protesting every movement. I'm pretty sure I'm okay, but I take things slow just in case. I flex my feet, move my legs, shake out the pain and stiffness in my arms and wrists.

Sore, but all good. Nothing's broken.

Something warm drips down the side of my cheek and I reach up, my eyes widening as I see the blood on my fingers.

Someone shouts my name. Unless I'm imagining things, which could be possible seeing how I just had the worst crash of my life.

"Emmy?" The shout echoes through the trees and I flinch as my head pounds from the sound. Even though I had my helmet on, it still hurts when you knock it against a rock.

I raise my hand and cringe at the pain that shoots through my arm, my shoulder, my neck. Not seriously hurt, but I think I might have whiplash.

"Emmy!" Someone rushes down the trail toward me and I groan. It's Cole. I don't want him to see me like this. When he reaches me, he kneels down and touches my face. "Emmy. Talk to me."

I take a breath to steady my breathing and close my eyes. "Go away."

He lets out a breath. "Good. You're talking, at least. Are you okay?"

I nod. "Yes." I flex my fingers again just to be sure. "I think anyway."

He stares at my forehead, his eyes wide. "You're bleeding." He unbuckles my helmet and takes it off my head, setting it down in the dirt next to him. I don't even protest.

"I know." I blush at the tender way he looks at me as I feel blood trailing into my eyebrow. "Where's my bike?"

He glances behind him and his face is pained when he looks back at me. He hesitates and opens his mouth, but I stop him.

"Don't tell me. I don't want to know. Not yet anyway." My baby is obviously broken. I spent so many hours building that bike. I don't know what I'll do if it's not fixable.

"It's not as bad as it could be. That's all I'll say right now." Before I know what he's doing, he's taking off his shirt.

"What . . ." I trail off. I'm perfectly aware I may have a concussion or something, but his chest is *really* nice to look at. Yep. I'm positive I have a concussion.

"The cut on your forehead is deep." He wads up the shirt and presses it to my forehead, making me flinch. "I'm pretty sure you need stitches."

"Great." I hold the shirt in place, despite it being covered in Cole's sweat. I don't know whether to be grossed out or a little turned on.

I take a breath, noting how it doesn't smell like sweat, though. It smells like him. A woodsy kind of smell. Whatever cologne he wears. Why would he wear cologne to a bike race?

I stare at him and curse myself. Why did I wear makeup?

Duh.

He gives me a strange look as he realizes I'm watching him. "You okay?"

"Yes. Thank you. Uh . . . for the shirt."

He looks around and then back at me. "We need to get you to the hospital. Can you stand?"

"I think."

He wraps his arm around my waist and lifts me to my feet. I wobble a little and cry out as I see my bike lying in the dirt a few feet away.

"What? What happened?" His voice is panicked. "What did I do?"

"Oh, no. No." I walk over to my bike and bend down, examining it. "My front wheel's bent."

He exhales a sigh of relief. "Don't do that! I thought I hurt you."

"No, you didn't hurt me. But look at this. Do you have any idea how long I saved up to get these?" I frown as I study my wheel. There's no way I'll be able to fix it.

Cole bends down next to me. "I'm sorry. That sucks."

"Yes. Yes it does. I bought these a few weeks ago." I sigh. Where the heck am I going get money for new wheels? There's no way Mom and Dad can lend me money, especially now that Mom . . .

I stare at the ground. Mom. She'll kill me when she finds out what happened. And worse, she'll kill me again for lying about Park City.

"Looks like your rear derailleur is messed up, too."

I glance at it. He's right. "Perfect." My day is officially ruined.

He picks up my bike and helps me to my feet again. "Come on. Let's head down the mountain. We need to get your head looked at." He pulls his phone out. "I'm calling Kelsie and letting her know what happened."

"I can talk to her." I can only imagine what she's going to do when she finds out I'm hurt.

"I've got it. Just try not to go into shock or something, okay?"

"I'm not going to go into shock."

He shoots me a look and walks my bike back up the hill until we get to his, sitting a few yards down the trail. He leans my bike against a tree, gibing me a look not to touch it, but I grab it with my free hand anyway.

"I can take it. I'm standing. I'm talking. I'm perfectly capable of walking my own bike down the hill."

He frowns as Kelsie answers her phone. "Kelsie? This is Cole. There's been a . . . yes. No, she's okay. Yes. No. She's bleeding, but she's . . . she's okay. Yes . . ."

I hear Kelsie's panicked voice on the other end and hope she doesn't do something stupid to try to get to me. I reach for the phone and Cole hands it over.

"Kels?"

"Emmy! What happened? Are you okay? Cole said you're bleeding. Do we need to call an ambulance? I'm sitting on the stupid ski-lift right now and it's taking forever to get me back down. Are you stuck up there? Can you get down yourself? What—"

"Kelsie. I'm okay. Cole's helping me down."

"I'll meet you in a second. Don't go into shock!"

I hang up and roll my eyes. "Sorry. She likes to freak out . . ."

He touches my shoulder to steady me as I trip over a rock. "Careful."

"Sorry."

He lets go of me, a deep crease in his forehead from frowning. "I'm not gonna lie—I sort of freaked out when I saw your bike without you on it. And when I saw you with the blood all over your face? Almost gave me a heart attack."

"I almost gave myself one." I suck in a breath as pain shoots through my head. At first I didn't feel it, but now . . . "I shouldn't have pulled on my brakes. I'm so stupid. I've never crashed in the three years I've been biking."

"You're not stupid."

"I am."

He's silent for a moment. "I'm glad you're not hurt worse. If something would have happened to you . . ." He trails off, and I let the emotion in his voice sink in.

"I'm fine. My bike's broken, but . . . I'm fine." I frown. "And Whitney won again."

"Don't worry about her right now."

"Okay. I promise I won't mention her again. Until I see her at the bottom, shouting how awesome she is to anyone who can hear."

"Deal." He nods and grabs the handlebars to my bike. "Why don't I walk yours, since it's injured." He gives me a smile. "And you walk mine."

"Okay." I take it and walk next to him, my frown deepening at the thought of the repairs I'm going to have to do because of one stupid mistake.

"I'm sorry, Emmy," he says.

"Don't be. This isn't your fault."

"Still."

I shake my head and sigh. It was *my* fault. I guess I don't know how to race.

Neither one of us says anything else.

CHAPTER 19

I've never been so afraid of calling my parents in my life.

"I'll do it if you want," Kelsie says. "They don't scare me." She stares out the window as I sit between her and Cole in his truck.

After my sad attempt at racing Whitney, she went off to celebrate her victory at some salon. She didn't even ask if I was okay. Not that I ever expected her to.

"They don't scare me either. I just . . . don't want to freak them out. Especially my mom." I don't want her to worry at all. She's got enough going on as it is. And secretly, I don't want her to ground me for the rest of my life.

"Why do you think they'll freak out?" Cole asks.

I give Kelsie a look and don't miss the tiny head shake she gives Cole. She knows I lied to Mom.

"They'll be fine," I mutter. Hopefully. I push the call button with one hand, while the other holds Cole's shirt on my head in place.

Dad answers. "Hey, Bug."

"Uh . . . hi." I'm glad Dad picked up, but I'm positive he's going to freak out as soon as I tell him what happened.

When I don't say anything, he asks, "Is everything okay?"

I hesitate. "Um . . . yes and no."

"Honey, what's wrong?" His voice is more panicked than before. I can just see him standing in the kitchen with his eyes wide.

"I kind of crashed riding my bike. I'm fine, but I'm pretty sure I need to get stitches."

"What? Where are you? I'm coming right now."

"In Park City."

"What? Why are you in Park City?"

"Uh . . . racing?"

He's silent and I squeeze my eyes shut. I hate disappointing Dad. "Did you tell Mom where you were going?"

"No. I . . . uh . . . told her I was going to Ogden."

More silence.

"I didn't want her to tell me I couldn't go. I'm sorry. Really." He won't say anything and now he's making me panic. I avoid Cole and Kelsie's concerned looks and focus on the dashboard in front of me. I try again. "Dad. I'm fine. It's not that bad, I promise."

I know he's standing with his fingers on the bridge of his nose, the way he looks when he's trying to control his temper. "Is anyone with you?"

"Yes."

"Who?"

"Kelsie and . . . Cole. I'm okay, Dad. It's a cut on my forehead. Not a big deal. More like a scratch." Ha. It's stinging so bad I want to cry.

Cole shoots me a look and shakes his head. It's definitely not a scratch.

"You're going to need insurance information. Do you have your card in your purse?"

"Yes."

"Okay. If the hospital needs anything else, call me back."

"I will."

"You come home right when you're done."

"Dad, I'm fine. I swear."

"I mean it, Emmy. We'll talk when you get home."

"Okay."

He hangs up.

I stare at the phone in my hand. Dad's never hung up on me before. He must be really mad. Which makes me feel even more awful.

When we pull into the parking lot of the hospital and Cole puts his truck in park, I sit there, my heart racing as I stare at the white building in front of me.

"You should probably put a shirt on, Cole," Kelsie says.

"Probably." He fishes in his biking bag and grabs one, pulling it over his head. I glance at him a moment and turn my attention back to the building. I don't want to go in there.

"Emmy? You okay?" Kelsie asks.

I don't answer, but keep my eyes on the hospital, remembering the last time I saw Lucas alive.

"Em." She reaches out and puts a hand on mine. "Let's go get you cleaned up, okay?"

I nod but don't say anything. Memories of Lucas are rushing back in, hitting me full force right now, and if I talk, the floodgates will open. So I clench my jaw and take my time walking up to the doors.

"You sure you're okay, Emmy?" Cole asks, worry creasing his brow.

"I'm fine."

They share a look, and I ignore them both.

We're in a totally different hospital than Lucas was in, but still. Everything smells the same. And the walls. White and plain. The same.

I bite my lip to keep myself under control.

Once I get checked in and put into a room, I wait for the doctor to come in.

"Have you ever gotten stitches before?" Cole asks.

I shake my head. "No." I stare at the floor.

"It's . . . not too bad." I glance up and by the look on his face, I know he's lying. "I got my first set of stitches when I was eleven. Slammed my finger in the door after I came home from school."

"Really?" Distraction from the pain. Keep talking, Cole.

"Yep. I had to get half my fingertip sewed back on. Went to school with a bunch of gauze and tape that made my finger look freaking huge."

I glance over at him and grin. "That would have scarred me for life seeing that."

"You should have seen underneath the gauze."

I shiver. "No thanks."

Kelsie shoots him a glare. "Not helping the situation."

"No, he's fine. I need him to keep talking. My head's killing me."

He folds his arms and leans against the wall. "Let's see. When was the last time you've been in the emergency room?"

"This is a first."

"Really? You've never had a broken bone or anything like that?"

"Nope."

He frowns. "First time for everything I guess."

He's got that right.

Eight stitches and a huge monster headache later, we're on our way home. After we left the hospital, we picked up Kelsie's car at the ski lodge.

Cole drives in front of us, my broken bike in the back of his truck. I don't want to think about my bike. If I would have been more careful, my wheels would be fine. But no. One rookie mistake.

I think of all the hours I put into that bike and try not to cry.

"You okay, Em? Need any more pain meds?"

"No." I'm tired. And I'm pretty sure I do need more pain meds. My head hurts and so does my pride, but I don't tell her that. I'm trying to be tough.

"I'm so sorry you crashed."

I sigh. "So am I."

Cole pulls into my driveway and takes my bike out of his truck. As he sets it on the ground in front of the garage, he looks at me. "If you need any help—"

"I'm fine," I say, a little too loud. "Thanks." All I want to do is go inside. Even if my parents are going to ground me forever, I'd rather be in my house, away from everyone else. "I'll see you guys later. Kelsie, thanks for bringing me home."

She gives me a hug and gets back in her car as I walk to my door.

"You sure you don't need anything?" Cole asks.

"No. Thanks for . . . bringing my bike back."

He shifts his weight and frowns, his arms folded.

I walk away from him. If he had any feelings for me before, they're probably gone now. He's seen me at my worst. In pain, exhausted, and almost passing out from stupid shots and stitches. And clearly I'm not the talented biker he thought I was.

Before I go inside, I look back at Cole. He's standing next to my garage, his arms folded and looking sad.

I open the door and leave him there alone.

CHAPTER 20

Of course my parents are waiting for me when I walk inside.

Dad's standing by the doorway to the kitchen and Mom's on the couch. As soon as I shut the door, Mom stands and wraps her arms around me. "You're okay?" I nod and she squeezes me once more before letting me go and taking a step back. "You sure?"

"Yes." I try to avoid her eyes, but it's hard when she's standing right in front of me.

Dad comes in the room, but stays back. "You're grounded forever."

"Dad," I start to protest.

Mom turns around and shakes her head at him, then she turns back to me. I flinch under her gaze. She's acting so normal. And looks calm. Too calm. Which means she's very angry. "I'm glad you weren't hurt worse." She pauses. "How many stitches?"

"Eight."

She nods and her gaze hardens. "So, eight weeks of grounding then?"

"Mom, no!"

She folds her arms. "Why did you lie to me?"

I shrug. "I didn't think you'd let me go."

"Why would you think that?"

"I know how you don't like me driving long distances very often."

She studies me, her eyes narrowed. "Still. You should have asked. I might have said yes this time. What if something worse would have happened to you? You're seventeen, Emmy. You live under my roof, so that means you obey my rules."

I sigh. I know. I know I was stupid. I made a mistake. I should say that, but I don't. I just stare at the floor, very aware of the pounding in my head and Dad glaring daggers at me from across the room.

"You're not going to say anything else?" she asks.

"No."

She lets out a breath, frustrated. "Emmy. You've never lied to me before. What's going on?"

"Nothing."

"Are you sure? Because this is so not like you."

I look away and grit my teeth to control my rising temper.

Dad takes a step toward us. "You know better, Emmy. Why would you deliberately break our trust?"

My head snaps up and my eyes narrow as I stare both of them down. "You want to talk about trust? What gives you the right to even bring that up?"

"Emmy," Dad warns.

"No. You two didn't tell me about Mom for six months. Six. Months. And you stand there and make me feel awful for not telling you about one stupid bike ride?"

164

"That's different, Emmy," Mom says. "It wasn't a lie. We just didn't tell you what was going on."

I fold my arms. "So you didn't tell me the truth, is what you're saying. And that makes it okay?"

She frowns and glances back at Dad for support. He walks over and joins her, putting an arm around her. He reaches out to touch me and I back up a step. "Bug, I realize now it wasn't okay not to tell you and Gavin. I'm sorry for that. We didn't want you to worry. We thought it wasn't a big deal at first."

"Wasn't a big deal? Mom's going to forget us!"

Mom's mouth drops open like I've slapped her. It takes her a moment to recover. "Honey . . ." She's shaking. Maybe trying not to cry. I know I'm doing the same thing.

Dad grabs her hand and speaks for her. "Mom's fine, Emmy. She's still Mom."

That's when I snap. "Why does everyone keep saying that? She's fine. She's fine. Oh, don't worry, she's fine. Why can't you tell me the truth? That she isn't fine. That she'll never be fine again. I looked up Alzheimer's disease. Do you know all the symptoms? Everything that's going to happen to her? I can't handle you saying she's fine anymore when you know perfectly well that she isn't."

Mom backs up a step, her mouth hanging open. It takes her a moment to find her voice, but she definitely finds it. "Emmy, we're not talking about me right now. We're talking about you. Why did you lie to us about your race? You could have told me the truth."

"You wouldn't have let me go."

"How do you know?"

"Because I know you."

She frowns. "I trust you, Emmy. But when you do stuff like this, it's hard for me to do that. You're grounded. No friends, no biking, nothing. For a week."

"What? No biking? You can't be serious!"

She nods, her eyes still on mine. "Yes, I am. No biking." She stares at me, frowns, glances at Dad, and steps out of my way.

"Emmy," Dad says, but I push past him and run downstairs. I slam the door, making my head ache worse, and slide down the door to sit on the floor. I pull my knees to my chest and bury my face in them.

This isn't fair.

CHAPTER 21

It's Monday. Two days since my stupid crash. I've been lounging around my room all day, but I don't care. My whole body hurts worse today than Saturday. So much so that I've barely left my room all weekend.

Lazy is the word of the day.

What am I supposed do if I'm grounded, though?

Nothing.

I throw a pile of clothes I've been sorting in the corner and push a few things under my bed to make it look like I've been cleaning. Like it will help at all. My room's a disaster.

Someone knocks and I assume it's Mom. I pinch my lips together and take a few deep breaths. I still haven't talked to her or Dad since our fight. I rock back on my knees and stare at the door, bracing myself for whatever Mom wants to talk to me about. "You can come in."

Gavin comes inside. "Hey."

I tilt my head, confused. "You knocked."

He shrugs. "Shocking, I know. I figured you might still be asleep since you haven't been feeling well lately." He plops himself down on my bed and looks me over. "You look . . . ready for the day."

I scowl at him and swipe my hair out of my face. "Yes. I know. I'm still in my pajamas. There's a first time for everything, right?"

"Uh . . . yes. Weird. It's . . ." He glances at my clock. "Almost six?"

"Yep."

"At night . . ."

"I know!" I lean back and rest my head and shoulders against the wall, giving him my best scowl.

"Just making sure you knew. How's your head?"

"Fine. I get my stitches out in a few days."

"Good." He picks up one of my biking gloves off the floor and turns it over in his hand. "So, I don't have to go to work for a few hours. You up for a movie? I know you're sore and don't feel the greatest, but I can even make some popcorn. Or go get us some treats. If you want."

I love the fact that he wants to spend time with me. But I can tell this isn't an average room call. He's worried about me. I can see it in his eyes. "Gav, are you ever going to ask a girl out instead of hanging with me every night?"

He throws my glove at me. "Girls are trouble."

"Well, duh. Of course we are. But still. You've gotta put yourself out there. You're cute and funny and—"

"Whoa!" He holds up his hand. "Sisters don't say that about brothers."

I chuckle. "I'm just telling you the truth. How long has it been since you've been on a date?"

He shrugs. "I don't really care right now. I'll just be spending money on someone else's wife."

Seriously? Can he be any more ridiculous? "Could be your future wife."

He snorts. "Right. Enough of the dating advice. You want to watch a movie or not?"

"Sure."

"Great." He stands and heads toward the door.

"Gav?"

He stops and turns around. "Yes?"

I bite my lip and pick at my fingernail, avoiding his eyes. "Are Mom and Dad still mad at me?"

He sighs. "Why don't you ask them?"

"I don't know."

"They're worried about you, Em. I am too."

I ignore that fact and put on a fake smile. "I'm fine."

"Sure you are. I know when my sister's having a hard time."

"Of course I am. I'm grounded."

His eyes narrow. "You know what I mean."

I let out a slow breath. "I know."

"Talk to me."

"I'm just stressed out about everything."

"Like?"

"Mom. Biking. Boys."

"Boys?"

"Lucas. I can't get past it. Still."

He walks over and sits down next to me. "Have you talked to anyone about it?"

I shake my head. "Not really."

"Maybe you should. You can talk to me."

I smile. "You don't want to hear about my boy problems."

"It's not just a boy problem. He was your best friend."

"I know." Not just my best friend. I could tell him anything—other than the fact that I was in love with him. I was always scared to tell him that. But everything else, he was always there to listen. Always there to tell me everything was going to work out.

"And Mom's still okay. Well enough to ground you anyway."

"Right."

"Have you talked to her about anything?"

"No."

"Maybe you should. She has a doctor's appointment tomorrow, maybe you should go with her."

I shake my head. "No." I'm not ready to do that. I'm not ready to hear it all from a doctor and have to accept the fact that she's sick. She should be taking me shopping or to dinner for a girls' night or going with me to see a movie and share a giant tub of popcorn. We haven't done anything like that for months. I miss it. So much. But I know I'm the one keeping us from it.

"Might be good for . . ." He trails off and shakes his head when he sees my face. "Never mind. I'll see you upstairs. If you can walk that far."

"Of course I can walk that far."

"Really? You haven't left your room in days. Have you even showered?"

Have I? I can't remember so I shrug. "Give me a minute to get dressed and I'll meet you up there."

"Sounds good." He leaves and then pokes his head back inside. "What do you want to watch?"

"Hmmm. I don't know. Maybe a chick flick?" I grin.

He rolls his eyes. "Seriously?"

"Knew you'd love that." I try to think of a movie I've been dying to see, but can't. "I don't care what we watch, as long as there's nothing super gory or scary."

He frowns. "You're no fun." The doorbell rings and he runs up the stairs. "Be right back."

I stare at the clothes on the floor and think about what Gavin said. Maybe I should apologize to Mom and Dad. I hate the tension. I hate feeling like this, but I don't know how to get over it. I don't know what I'm supposed to be feeling. As for talking to someone about Lucas . . . I've talked Kelsie's ear off. Who else would I be able to talk to about him? And why does he think it will help?

I look up as Gavin comes back in my room a few minutes later, a bunch of daisies in his hand.

"What's that?"

He gives me a wicked grin and hands them to me. "For you."

I take them from him and pluck the card out of the bouquet.

Emmy,
Get Well Soon.
Cole

My eyes narrow as I read the note again. "Really? Get well soon? That's all he could think of?"

"I'm not really one to write notes."

My breath catches as I recognize the voice. I turn toward the door to see Cole stepping inside, with Gavin nowhere to be seen. My face flames. "What . . . what are you doing down here? Where's Gavin?"

"He's on his way upstairs. I told him I'd buy him dinner if he let me in to talk to you, since he said you didn't want to see anyone. Me especially."

I frown. That wasn't totally true. I never said I didn't want to *see* him. But talking to him is a totally different story. "He's never been good with bribes. Especially when it involves food. I'm surprised you knew that." I run my hand over my face, trying to wipe the sleep from my eyes and curse myself for not having changed out of my pajamas.

"I didn't know that actually. I guess he can't pass up a good meal. And I figured he took after you." He studies my face and shoves his hands in his pockets. "I'll leave if you want me to."

I hesitate and can't help but stare at him. He's in jeans and a yellow polo. His hair is spiked and gelled like it usually is, but there's something different about him. His expression is solemn, sad even.

Why is he here?

Cole eyes the floor where I'm sitting and my heart speeds up. "Can I sit down?" I try to decide if I should stay where I am on the floor or move to the window seat. Or the bed. No. The bed would be weird. And the window seat would be weird, too. I stay where I am.

"Emmy?"

Still staring. A million thoughts running through my head. *Pull yourself together, Emmy. Say something.*

He takes my silence as a yes, I think, because he takes a step closer and glances at the flowers in my hand. I set them on the floor next to me. He picks his way through my messy room (right now I'm really wishing I would have listened to Mom and cleaned it earlier) and stops right in front of me.

He only hesitates a second before sitting cross-legged on the floor next to me. He smiles as he looks around the room for a second, his eyes glued to the wall across from us. "Nice posters."

"Uh . . . thanks." I stare at him, not knowing what else to say. "Um . . . thanks for the flowers."

"You're welcome."

It takes me a minute, but I finally find myself. At least for now. "I'm sure you send flowers to every girl, so I won't think anything of it."

He laughs. "It's good to hear you're still the same." He shakes his head. "And you should know I don't send flowers to girls. Ever. Feel special, okay?"

My cheeks redden. "Okay." I bite my lip and twist my ring. "So . . . why are you here? Do you need something?"

"I don't have to need something to want to see you, Emmy."

I don't know what to say to that, so I settle with, "Oh." My fingers stop twisting my ring, and I glance over at him.

His eyes are darker today. Flecks of brownish gold spiral around his pupil, making the green pop more than usual. I wish my eyes changed color like his do in the light. Cole's mouth twitches and breaks into a small smile. I look away, embarrassed that he caught me staring at him. Again.

He clears his throat. "I wanted to come by to tell you how sorry I am about the crash the other day. I shouldn't have talked you into racing Whitney again. Especially in Park City. That trail is rough. And I shouldn't have pressured you about captain. I don't blame you if you don't want to ever talk to me again, since your bike is ruined. I know how hard you worked on it. I'm just . . . sorry. For everything."

He's apologizing. To me. My life is so backwards. I haven't been nice to him this entire time and he's the one trying to make amends. My life is so screwed up. "Cole. It wasn't your fault."

"It was." He looks down at his hands, twisted in his lap. "If it wasn't my fault, why didn't you want to talk to me again?"

I smile in spite of myself. "If it's one thing I'm good at, it's pushing people away. The fact that I lost to Whitney . . . again, kind of put a damper on things." I fold my arms. "I was mad. At myself mostly. I have a hard time admitting defeat."

"You didn't lose. Whitney didn't really finish the race."

"What?" I frown.

"She thought she heard you fall, so she stopped a little ways down the trail. When she didn't see you coming, she called me."

"She called you? Why?"

He looks at me like I've lost my mind. "She's not as evil as you think she is. And she thought you were hurt."

"If it was a normal race, she wouldn't have stopped."

"How do you know?"

I stare at him, trying to figure him out. "I don't."

"Like I said, she's not that bad." He adjusts the watch around his wrist before looking at me again. "Also. Is there a reason you're still so short with me? Besides captain, have I ever done anything else to piss you off? Because that's how you talk to me. All the time. Like you're pissed at me. It's kind of . . . well . . . getting old."

"I really do?" I whisper.

He snorts. "Um . . . yes. To be honest, I'm not sure why I'm still trying. I almost didn't come over here. I'm ready to give up on you."

The look on his face confirms his words. He's serious. I really am a brat. And right now, I feel awful. "I'm . . . sorry, Cole. I hate feeling like this. So . . . wound up and trapped in my screwed-up emotions. I'm just having a hard time right now. And I'm not sure why I chose to take things out on you. You've been nothing but nice to me and I . . ."

"I get it. A little. It's the other guy. Lucas. You're still in love with him." I shake my head, but he just smiles. "I can see it. It's okay. You're grieving still. And then I come along and—"

"Make things complicated." I twist my hands in my lap and try my hardest not to look at him. I fail.

175

"Yeah." He smiles. "Sorry about that. I guess. Well, I have a proposal. Again. Nothing to do with Lucas or anything. I promise."

"Okay?"

"I want to start over. Push aside the whole captain thing. I want you to get to know me for real. I'm the bad guy in your eyes, but it's because you don't know anything about me. You've only heard the rumors."

"Cole—"

He holds up a hand. "We'll start small, I swear. Since you really want to win the Back Country race in a few weeks, I was wondering . . . if you're feeling up to it in a few days, do you want to train with me? And I swear I'm not saying I'm better than you or anything. I've just watched you race and I . . . I think I could help you out a little. Whitney's good, Em. Really good. Which gives her an advantage over you in the Back Country. But with the right motivation and a few tricks, you could take her."

I stare at him. Do I dare let Cole teach me? Like a real coach? I really could use some pointers. "Maybe?" I squeak. Our school coach, Coach Clarke, is really nice, but the only reason he's our coach is because we begged him to help us get a team together since we had to have an adult to supervise. He's not a professional biker, just a track coach who wanted to help us out. So this—a *real* coach—this would be new.

"Maybe?" He cocks an eyebrow. "If I threw in a few shakes, would you say yes?"

"What makes you think a food bribe would work on me?"

He laughs. "It worked for your brother, so I thought I'd give it a try."

I try to stop the grin from creeping to my face. "Maybe one shake would be okay. I guess."

"Why don't I go grab one and we can watch a movie or something. If that's okay. I don't want to invite myself over. It's just . . . I'd like to hang out with you today. If you're okay with it, of course. Because it's something small to start with. Maybe we can have a conversation without you insulting me."

My lips twitch. "Sure. I'd like that."

"Great. I have to run to the store for my dad real quick, so I'll pick up a few shakes on the way back."

"That sounds great." Shower. Change of clothes. Makeup. Stat.

He stands. "I'll see you in an hour or so then."

I stay where I am. I don't want him to see the full ensemble I'm wearing. I look less than awesome in my holey pajama pants. "Okay."

It's only after he leaves, I realize how messy my room really is. Oh well. At least my underwear isn't on the floor. Or is it? I glance around to make sure. No. None. Phew.

After the front door slams upstairs, Gavin pokes his head back in my room. "I'm guessing the movie is a no-go."

"Oh, Gav, I'm sorry!"

He laughs. "No worries. I'll crash your movie *date* instead. You need a chaperone anyway."

"It's not a date."

"Whatever."

That's when I remember I'm still grounded. Maybe Gavin would cover for me . . .

CHAPTER 22

Cole comes over an hour later. I take a quick look in the mirror in the bathroom, feeling refreshed from my shower. I'm ready. Not sweaty from a bike ride or looking like I just rolled out of bed. I look . . . nice. Hair done, makeup on. Actually dressed in jeans and a nice shirt. Something about seeing Cole makes me want to look at least a little presentable.

Which makes me wonder how that happened. One day, he was the cocky self-absorbed mountain biking playboy, and now? I can't get him out of my head.

I jog upstairs and head for the kitchen. Dad passes by and glances inside. "You going somewhere tonight? Because I'm pretty sure you're still grounded."

"Not going anywhere. Someone's coming here, if that's okay."

His eyes narrow and he stands there as though he's deep in thought. "Okay. As long as you stay here, it's fine. But you can't leave."

"Thanks." We stare at each other a moment, each not knowing what to say. We haven't talked since I blew up the other night, and every time I've seen him or Mom, I've taken every measurable step to avoid it. But right now, I'm kind of missing them. Both of them. Especially Mom. "I'm sorry again, Dad. For not telling you or Mom where I was going."

His expression softens. "I know."

"I won't do it again."

"Let's hope not."

I fiddle a strand of hair, twisting it around my finger. "Where's Mom tonight?"

He glances down the hallway toward their room. "She's . . . not having the best night. She put her two weeks in at work today."

"What? Why? She loves her job."

He shakes his head. "She can't do it anymore. She's made too many mistakes the past few months and knows if she stays, someone could get hurt. If she wouldn't have put her two weeks in, they would have let her go anyway."

"I'm sorry, Dad."

"It's okay. We knew it was coming. We weren't expecting it to be this soon, though. The doctor said she'd be okay for a while, but now . . ." He trails off and lets out a slow breath. I want to hug him and tell him everything will be okay, even though it won't. "Have fun tonight, okay?" He pats me on the back and leaves me alone.

I step through the doorway into the hall and watch him walk to his bedroom. He closes the door once he's inside. Mom's in there, I'm sure. I should go talk to her. Tell her it's okay she's quitting her job. But I know it won't do any good. I'm sure she's devastated.

I open the fridge to find something to eat and try to think of something happy, but can't focus on anything other than my life unraveling. What if Dad doesn't make enough for Mom to quit? How will we afford to live?

When the doorbell rings, Gavin answers it and I hear Cole talking. Once they've laughed a few times, I decide to join them.

"Have fun, you two," Gavin says. "And remember. I'll be watching." He winks at me as he goes in the other room.

I'm going to short sheet his bed tonight.

"Brought you something," Cole says. He pulls a stack of DVDs out of a bag. "I'm not sure what you like to watch, so I brought a bunch of different genres." He sets them on my lap and digs into his bag again.

"*The Hobbit* and *Lord of the Rings*?"

"I wasn't sure if that was one you liked, but . . . I'm kind of obsessed. I know some girls aren't into it, so it's fine if you choose something else."

I stare at the cover and smile. "Something you should know about me: Legolas is my boyfriend."

"Oh. Good to know I'll be competing with an elf with girl hair."

I laugh. "His hair *is* pretty dreamy." I flip through the other movies and settle on a romantic comedy I haven't seen. When I hand it to him, he takes it without complaint. "But for real. I love *Lord of the Rings*. The only reason I'm not choosing it is because I have to watch the extended versions and that would take way too long." I glance at him and smile as he produces a carton of ice cream from a plastic bag. "You brought ice cream?"

He shrugs. "I thought about a shake and then had a better idea." He pulls out bananas, chocolate and caramel syrup, whipped cream, and sprinkles.

"Holy crap. It's an ice cream bar! You're my favorite!"

"I knew I'd change your mind about me."

My cheeks heat. "A little. Don't get too carried away. Maybe I'll change my mind more if you tell me another truth."

"Maybe. If I decide to tell one."

"Oh, I'll get at least one out of you."

"Ha!"

I'm surprised by how comfortable I'm getting with him. It's different than before—than even two hours earlier. Now that I know how awful I was to him. No arguing, no trying to be better than him. I'm just . . . me.

"You ready to start the movie or do you want the ice cream first?"

"Ice cream. For sure."

I grab the toppings and he gets the ice cream as we head into the kitchen. He watches as I get two bowls and spoons out of the dishwasher and set them on the table.

"I make a mean banana split," he says.

"You can do the honor then."

"Do you have a knife?"

I grab one out of the drawer and hand it to him, curious.

"The bananas are better when they're cut up into slices."

"Oh. Good to know." I don't know how long it's been since I've had a banana split. Years, probably.

I sit down and watch him work. The way he cuts all the bananas in perfect slices, the tip of his tongue peeking through his very kissable lips.

My heart speeds up at that thought. What would it be like to kiss him? I shake my head and stare at the container of sprinkles in front of me to distract myself.

"And voila," he says. He scoots the bowl in front of me and waits for my reaction.

I look at his masterpiece. "This looks delicious."

"Told you."

I take a bite and after I wipe the whipped cream off my face, I stand. "Let's start the movie then."

I put the movie in and take my place on the couch. Cole sits down next to me. We aren't touching, but we're close.

The movie isn't too bad. In fact, I find myself laughing through most of the beginning. We finish our banana splits and he takes them back into the kitchen. When he comes back, I notice he sits closer to me this time. We're separated by an inch or so.

A big part of me wants him to close the gap, and the voice in my head, the one still holding on to Lucas, shouts at me to move away.

I ignore the voice.

Toward the end of the movie, I feel my eyes drooping. Cole scoots closer and, after hesitating only a second, puts his arm around me. "You're tired," he says.

"Yes." I didn't realize how tired I am until now and decide to be brave. Or maybe stupid. Or maybe I'm so exhausted that the rational part of my brain turns off as I lean my head on his shoulder.

The movie plays, and I tune it out, my eyes closed, but ears still listening. When it ends, I open my eyes, which I'm sure are bloodshot from my contacts being in for too long, but I don't want him to leave yet. I like being with him. I like the feeling of his arm around me. And that freaking terrifies me.

He nudges my shoulder. "You still out?"

"I never fell asleep," I say, almost slurring.

"You were snoring."

I sit up, praying I wasn't drooling, too. "Was not."

He chuckles. "No, you weren't." I study his eyes to make sure he's not lying. I don't think he is. "I promise you didn't snore."

Sigh of relief. "Good." I've been known to snore. That's why I was worried. It totally could have happened.

Cole squeezes my shoulder as I move around to try and get comfortable. "This was fun. Next time I choose the movie, though."

"Blood and guts it is," I tease.

"Eh. I'm not a huge fan of all that."

"Neither am I. Besides *Lord of the Rings*, of course."

He smiles. "Of course." He hesitates before reaching out a hand to take mine. "Is this okay?"

After a moment's hesitation, I nod.

He squeezes my hand in response. "So, a truth."

"What?"

"I'm going to tell you a truth. I believe the last time I told you one was when I took you on that date."

"Yes. I believe you're right." It was the first time I saw him as more than just a playboy. Maybe the first time I kind of felt something for him.

"Okay. Here goes." He lets out a long, exaggerated breath. "I'm terrified of spiders."

My mouth drops open. "You're kidding."

He grins. "Not at all." His teeth are really white in the dim light. And straight. I wonder if he had to have braces when he was younger. He'd look cute in braces.

"Are you serious?"

"When I see one in the house, my mom has to come kill it for me. Unless it's on the floor. I'll step on it then."

"So, ceiling spiders are a no-go."

He shivers. "The worst. They could fall on me and I'd never know where it landed."

I throw my head back and laugh, then glance at the hallway to make sure my parents didn't wake up. "That's hilarious," I whisper. "I never thought you'd be afraid of something as dumb as a spider."

"Do you like them?"

"I wouldn't let one crawl on me or anything, but I don't go all crazy and kill one if I see it. Unless it's a huge one with babies on its back. Ew. I get Gavin to take care of those."

He shivers again. "So there's my truth. Let's hear one from you."

"Hmmm . . ." I wrack my brain with ideas, but I'm not sure which one to tell him. "I love food."

"So I've heard."

"I don't eat a ton, but I do love the taste of food. I like to savor each bite. Especially if it's something I really like. Like pie. Or ice cream."

"So you have a sweet tooth then. Noted."

I lean forward a little more, our faces a few inches from each other. We're so close, I could move a tad more and touch his lips. I've already noticed that he has nice lips. And I'm positive he's a good kisser. He's got to be. "So, if I ask you a question, will you answer truthfully?"

"Depends on the question."

"Understandable."

"Do you have a question to ask?"

I shrug. "Maybe."

"Shoot."

"Why, after a year of me being awful to you, did you not give up trying to be my friend?"

His eyes sparkle in the lamp light as he stares at me. "I only said one truth tonight."

"You don't have to answer if you don't want to."

"No, I'll answer." He smiles and rubs his thumb in little circles on the back of my hand, making me shiver. "I've had a crush on you since the first time I walked into one of your biking meetings."

"It was a serious question. Quit flirting with me."

"I'm not."

"That's not true. Is it?" My cheeks flame and I try to pull away from him, but he doesn't let go.

"I'm serious. Your hair was pulled in a ponytail, your eyes were bright and focused when you talked about what the team needed to work on. I could see the passion in every movement you made, explaining what races we were going to tackle and what not. And your voice. Don't get me started on that." He gives me a wicked grin. "Sexy."

I burst out laughing and then cover my mouth. I swear my parents are going to come in the room any second. And then Dad would kick Cole out because it's almost midnight. Or maybe they'd let him stay. I don't bring friends home very often. Besides Kelsie. "My voice is not sexy."

"Is too. It's kind of lower. It's nice."

"Stop talking," I say, blushing furiously.

"You wanted me to answer your question, so I did."

"No you didn't. You didn't really answer it. You said you had a crush on me. Why did you keep trying to be my friend after I quit the team?"

I expect him to make another joke, but he doesn't. Instead, his eyes find mine and his expression softens. "Because at the beginning of the school year, underneath the passion and love for mountain biking I saw a girl who needed someone to care about her."

"What?"

"You appear confident, like you don't have any cares or worries, but deep down you're not. Ever since your Lucas died, you push people away."

I stare at him, trying to make sense of what he's saying. It's a truth I don't want to admit.

He squeezes my hand, and I pull it away. "Why do you push people away, Emmy? Why don't you get close to anyone?"

"I'm close to plenty of people."

"Name two." He looks at me, his expression serious. "Besides your brother and Kelsie."

I look away.

"Tell me about him."

"Who?"

"Lucas."

"I can't."

"I met him once."

"When?"

"At that carnival fundraiser for him last year. He seemed cool."

"He was."

"So, tell me something about him. A nice memory. Talk about him. I want to know what he was like."

My eyes fill with tears, and I try to blink them back. Why does he want to know about him so bad?

"Emmy."

I take a shaky breath. I don't know if I want to tell him, but it comes pouring out anyway. "We grew up together. Me, Lucas, and his sister, Oakley."

He nods, but waits for me to continue.

"We were inseparable. Lucas was two years older than me, and Oakley was a year. But it didn't matter. We hung out all the time."

"I've heard the name Oakley. People have talked about her at school. They said she just left town before graduation and never came back."

I don't want to know what everyone's said about her. The good or the bad, so I keep talking. "She graduated early." I pause a moment, gathering my thoughts. "I used to watch Lucas play basketball in his front yard when we were growing up. He was good. On the school team and everything. He was basically one of those people who was good at whatever he tried. I played with him in his driveway sometimes, and embarrassed myself, and he'd come biking with me other times. That's when I discovered mountain biking was the one thing he *wasn't* good at." I smile at the memory of him freaking out when I went down a hill faster than him. "We hung out a lot after school, played video games, went to get shakes, but most days we just sat around talking for hours. He was there for me when I had bad days, and I was there for him when he did. The times where he broke up with girlfriends and the times I didn't get along with my parents. Like I said. We were really close.

"When his cancer came back, he told me everything was going to be okay, even though we both knew he wasn't going to make it." I sniff, holding back tears. "He should have been fine. He shouldn't have had to go through so much pain. It's not fair."

I stare at our hands entwined and then close my eyes. Cole's not Lucas. He's not Lucas. He's not like him at all actually. But why do I feel like I can tell him things? Why do I think I can trust him?

He's watching me. He doesn't bug me to finish, just sits there, waiting.

"It's funny how life works out sometimes. Lucas and I never dated, but I always loved him from afar. He had girlfriends all through high school. How couldn't he, since he was so . . . perfect. And Oakley worshipped her brother. They were best friends.

"When he knew he didn't have much time left, he asked me to come to the hospital. He told me . . ." I swallow the lump in my throat and Cole squeezes my hand. "He told me he loved me. That he was sorry he never acted on it earlier. That he regretted telling me so late."

I think of the moments we shared. The look on his pale face. The intense feeling of regret that I never kissed him or held his hand, and how we could have been together and happy. It was too much for my sixteen-year-old heart to take.

"He died a week later. And everything fell apart after that. Oakley didn't talk to me again. Her parents separated and then she moved to California with her mom. I know she wasn't mad at *me*, but it still hurt when she left without saying good-bye."

"Have you talked to her since then?"

"Yes. A few times on the phone, which is good. She's doing well and just got engaged to a nice guy named Carson."

"Isn't she our age? That's super young."

"She's a year older than me. And yeah, it's young. But when it's right, it's right, I guess." I wonder if I'll ever meet him. I hope so. "I'm happy for her. She deserves to be happy after all she went through with her brother."

"She does. You deserve to be happy, too, you know."

I shrug. "When I realized he wasn't going to make it, and especially after he passed away, I stopped letting myself get close to people. I don't know why. It was a coping thing,

I guess. If I don't get close, people can't hurt me, right? It kind of lingered and got worse as the year went on. It's one reason I quit the biking team. Not all, since you were a huge part of it. And Whitney joining. But . . . yeah. There you go. That's my story. I have issues, I guess. And now that my mom's having problems . . ." My eyes widen and I stop talking. Why would I tell him that?

"Your mom?"

I shake my head. "Nothing."

"You can tell me, Em. You can trust me. I promise."

"I know . . . I don't want to get into that right now. Maybe some other time."

He smiles and squeezes my hand. "I'll be here if you need me."

"I know."

"I'm sorry for everything you've gone through."

I smile. "Not your fault."

"I know. But still, it sucks."

"It does."

He's quiet for a moment before he speaks again. "My sister ran away from home when she was fifteen. I was thirteen. We were really close. Did everything together, believe it or not. When she was a sophomore in high school, she got mixed up in the wrong crowd. Got hooked on some pretty bad drugs and things. Her and my parents fought all the time. Then one day, she just left." He shakes his head. "I didn't see her for years."

"I'm sorry. Have you seen her since then?" I can't imagine something like that happening to Gavin.

He shrugs. "She's in rehab right now, doing better I think. She doesn't contact the family very often. There's still a lot of tension between her and my parents. I just wish . . . I could have done something. Anything to help her make better choices than she did. I mean, I wasn't a saint, but she knew better. She knew what drugs would do to her and she still did it. She was such a good girl."

"Sometimes people make crappy choices, but it doesn't mean they're bad. It just takes them a bit longer to realize their mistakes and get back on track with the rest of us."

"I know. Learn from our mistakes, I guess."

"Yes. And I'm not saying I'm perfect. We all have things we need to work on. Some are just different than others."

He squeezes my hand. "Thanks. For that."

"You're welcome."

As we sit there together, I feel safe. Like we've made some progress on the whole trust thing. I do trust him. And even though I miss Lucas and thought I knew what love was when I was with him, I can't help but feel like I'm going to be okay. That I'll figure things out and let people into my life again.

When Oakley and Lucas left, they left two gaping holes in my heart. Holes I didn't think could be filled again. But Kelsie stepped in and took care of one. Maybe Cole will fill the other.

For right now, though, as I sit next to him and lean my head on his shoulder, all I can think of is how happy I am that he didn't give up on me. And hopefully I'll continue to let him in.

CHAPTER 23

Instead of my alarm going off the next morning, Mom's knock wakes me up. "Hey, Emmy. I'm heading to work and wanted to make sure you were feeling okay." She motions toward the stitches in my head, and I nod.

"I'm fine." I blink a few times, trying to wake up, and as I take in her appearance, I frown. She looks tired. There are splotches on her face, too, like she's been crying. As I think back on my conversation with Dad about her putting in her two weeks, I'm positive she has been. She loves her job. I'm sure she's having a hard time with this decision.

It makes me feel ten times worse that I've been avoiding her.

"Those flowers are beautiful. Did a boy give them to you?"

I glance at my nightstand at the daisies Cole brought. "Maybe."

"Looks like this one's a keeper."

"Sure." I really don't want to discuss Cole with her right now because I don't know what he is to me. Or what I want him to be.

"Good. Do you have any plans today?"

"I might go biking." On what, I'm not sure, since my stupid wheel is broken.

"Go with someone, please. I don't want you to get hurt again with no one to help you."

I sigh. "I know."

She comes into my room and sits on my bed. "It looks a little better in here." She cringes as she sees the pile of clothes stacked in the corner.

"It looks the same. I think."

"Yes, pretty much." She laughs and so do I.

"You should be used to it by now. I've been this way my whole life."

She pats my arm. "It doesn't mean you can't change."

"I know." I really should work on being cleaner. My biking stuff is all organized and perfect, but for some reason I can't get a hold of keeping my room clean. "I think I take after Dad."

She laughs. "Of course you do." She stares at my posters on the wall and, for a moment, I feel like everything's fine. She's still my mom. She still knows who I am. My world isn't crashing down anymore. "So what do you want to do for girls' night next week?"

I shrug. "I don't know. Maybe see a movie? That might be nice."

She's silent.

"Mom?"

Silence again. She is still staring at one of my posters.

"Mom," I say again, getting out of bed and crouching in front of her. "Mom. Are you okay?"

She blinks and stares at me a second before looking around. "Oh. Yes." She looks around like she's seeing me for the first time. "Yes, I'm fine. Sorry, I just . . . lost my train of thought for a second." She chuckles. "What were we talking about?" She hesitates. "Girls' night, right?"

"Yes. I said we should go see a movie or something."

"That sounds great." She stands.

I bite my lip as she puts a hand on my shoulder. "You're sure you're okay, Mom?"

"Yes. Don't stay in bed all day, okay?"

"Okay."

As I listen to her retreating footsteps, I take slow, deep breaths and as soon as I shut the door I pick up the closest thing to me and throw it across the room.

I cringe as the glass in the picture frame shatters all over the floor and I stand there, breathing hard until I realize what I've done. I take a few careful steps, hoping I don't step on any glass, and stare down at the now crinkled and bent picture on the floor. The broken frame lies on the picture and covers Mom's face. All I see are Dad, Gavin, and myself staring back at me.

It may as well be my soon-to-be future.

Without Mom.

CHAPTER 24

Determined to do something besides think about Mom, I decide to fix my bike. I clean up the glass mess in my room, get ready for the day, and go shopping. After a quick stop at the bike shop, the second-hand store, and about a hundred bucks later, I have a new rear derailleur. But unfortunately no new wheels.

My music blasts in the garage as I work on my Gary Fisher, and I don't even notice the huge truck pull into my driveway until Cole's tapping me on the shoulder.

I about jump out of my skin. "Holy—"

He steps back. "Sorry about that."

I put my hand over my heart and take a deep breath. "No worries. You just . . . scared me."

"What ya working on?" He grins and leans over to my shoulder to see my handiwork.

"Just a bike. I'm getting ready to sell it."

"This is the one you were working on last week, right? Looks good."

"Thanks."

He rocks back on his heels. "So . . . I kind of have something to show you."

I wipe my greasy hands on my pants and stand. "What?"

He nods his head for me to follow him and leads me around his truck. "Close your eyes."

Really? "Okay." He grabs my hand and pulls me forward. I smile as I feel his hand in mine and think of last night. Being so close to him. A few seconds later, he lets go of my hand and moves his to my shoulder. "You can open your eyes."

I do as he says and raise my eyebrows at what's sitting in front of me. My mouth drops open and I look over at him. "A new wheel set?"

He nods. "I thought you could use some new ones since you kind of beat your other ones up."

I stare at the wheels. The beautiful, shiny rims. I know for a fact how expensive they are. The brand name says it all. After taking them in and maybe drooling a little, I manage to shake my head. "I can't take these."

"It's not a big deal, Em. I know how much you want to win that race. I also know how much money you need for new wheels. And since it was my fault you crashed—"

"Like I said before, not your fault."

He rolls his eyes. "Still. I wanted to make it up to you." He takes a step closer and grabs my hand. "So . . . take them. Please."

I don't know why I want to cry, and it takes quite the effort to hold the tears back. He shouldn't be so nice to me, especially when I've done nothing to deserve it. There has to be a catch, doesn't there?

"I promise it's okay." He smiles and leans forward, kissing me on the cheek. Before I can do anything, or react, he leans back. I raise my hand, touching the spot he kissed, and can't help but grin. Two seconds ago, I was fighting tears and now I can't wipe the smile off my face. What is he doing to me?

He keeps talking, oblivious to my reaction. "And if you don't like them, or you'd rather have something else, I'll take them back and you can pick your own. I know you have different taste than me."

I can't help it. I take a step forward and hug him. He doesn't even hesitate before wrapping his arms around my waist. I like it here. It's . . . safe. "They're amazing. I don't really have words. Thank you is the only thing I can think of, and I know it's not enough. How in the world did you afford these?"

"I do some work for my uncle sometimes when he needs an extra hand."

"Doing what?"

"Landscaping."

"Oh. I didn't know that."

He chuckles. "Well, now you do."

I shouldn't take them. The rational part of me wouldn't. I like working for things, and I don't need anyone's charity. But his gesture is so unexpected. So . . . nice. I can't say no. Not when he's looking at me the way he is.

I pull away from him, a shy smile on my face.

"Thank you is perfect." He watches as I lean down to pick up the wheels and look them over.

"Perfect size and everything." I want to hug him again, but I restrain myself.

"See? I pay attention to things." He grins.

"That you do."

"Shall we put them on and go for a ride?"

"I'd love to."

"Great. Let's get to work and try them out."

It's funny how things change. A few weeks ago, I wouldn't have given Cole the time of day. And now as we get our gear on at the beginning of the trail, I realize how bad I misjudged him. Sponsor and all.

"So," I say, glancing at his gloves and new helmet. "Edge gives you gloves and whatever gear you need to ride? Do you have to wear it to races to show off their logo or what?"

"Pretty much." He pulls on his gloves and flexes his fingers. "It's all about the name." I nod, noting everything he's wearing has Edge on it. "The only bad thing, is if I want to try another brand, I can't. At least not at a race. I have to wear their stuff at all times or I could get fined."

"Interesting." I don't know if I could ever afford Edge equipment. It's all super expensive. I get by with my knock-off brands. And really? I'm okay with it.

"They wanted me to go on tour all summer, but I told them I couldn't yet. I had some things I needed to take care of first." He stares at me for a second and then turns his attention to putting on his helmet. I really hope he didn't say no because of me. I'd feel horrible. "I'm leaving in July for a few weeks to bike a few different places around the west coast."

"Oh?" I'm surprised at the sudden drop in my stomach. He *is* leaving then. Boo.

"I leave on the fifteenth."

"That sounds . . . fun." I try to hide my sudden disappointment, but I'm pretty sure he catches it.

"Don't worry. You won't miss me that much."

I glare at him and he chuckles.

"You ready?"

I nod and swing my leg over my bike. "When you are."

He adjusts his CamelBak and pushes a button on his GPS hooked to his handlebars. "Okay. I'm teaching you a few tricks, nothing huge, since you're pretty much awesome already, but a few things you may not have known teaching yourself."

He starts riding, and I follow right next to him. "When you're going to shift gears to go up a hill, I've noticed you do it right as the bike starts up the hill. That's what you don't want to do. You want to shift into a lower gear as you approach the hill. If you shift into a lower or higher gear as you hit the hill, you could snap your chain. Especially if you're in the middle of a race and going really fast."

We approach a hill, and I shift down to one before we start up. My mouth drops open at how much easier it is to climb. "How did I not know that?"

He shrugs. "You taught yourself."

"I was captain of the team, though. I should have known something like that. Or someone should have told me."

"Well, if you don't have a coach to tell you things, which, when you started your biking club, you didn't, you have to figure it out yourself. I had a coach back in California for years. And don't feel bad. That's such a little mistake riders make that not a lot of them even think about it until they're stranded with a snapped chain in the middle of a trail. Or race."

I switch into a lower gear as we approach a hill, and once I start the climb, I'm surprised at how smooth the ride is. It's not as . . . jarring, I guess.

"See? Nice and easy," he says at the top.

"That really was a lot better."

"Now. When I trained in Cali, my coach taught me three things you need if you want to be a racer: Patience. Endurance. Drive."

"Patience?" That one's going to be a problem. I'm not a patient person. Never have been.

He must see my expression because he chuckles. "Yes. Patience. You don't want to burn out too fast when you're racing. Especially at the beginning of the race. I usually stay at the front of the pack, second or third, and make my move as I get closer to the finish line. You know how hard it is to pass people when you're exhausted. Save your energy and then push yourself at the end and wait for the right opening. Whoever's in the lead will be surprised when you go by and have to work even harder to pass you again. You know exactly what I mean, right? You've been near the end of a race before and know how hard it is to catch up, even if you're only a few seconds behind."

"Yes. I do that a lot actually," I grumble as I think of Whitney's pink spandex passing me like I'm tied to a pole.

"Okay, so patience. Huge. Now, second thing? Endurance. You ready to ride again?"

I nod, and we start out slow, me riding next to him as long as the trail stays wide.

"You have to push yourself. Every time you go biking, don't ride up here for fun. I mean, you can sometimes, but if you're really training for a race, push yourself to get a better time. It helps to eat better, drink lots of water to keep hydrated, and push your body to its limit to make it get used to using all your stored-up energy. I especially want you to work on climbing."

I squeeze my handlebars tight. He knows I'm not the best climber. As much as I want to argue with him, I don't.

"Last thing is drive. Be in it to win it. And I know you want to win it."

The way he says it makes me laugh. "I do."

He grins. "Right on. Let's try out those new wheels of yours and see how far I can push you today." Thoughts of leisure riding are gone as he puts on the speed and takes off in front of me. He calls over his shoulder. "Keep up if you can!"

I clench my jaw, squeeze my handlebars even harder, and push after him.

CHAPTER 25

My body is killing me. No wonder Cole got a sponsor; he's a maniac on wheels.

"You doing okay, Em?" He stands a few feet away, concern etching his face.

"I'm fine." I lean over the edge of the trail and rinse out my mouth with some water, spitting it into the bushes below. I wasn't planning on throwing up today, but . . . yeah. That happened.

And when I throw up, it's not some dainty sound. I'm pretty sure the entire valley below us heard it. I wouldn't be surprised if someone thought a murder was happening up here. And I really wish I was exaggerating. I'm not.

I stand up straight on shaky legs and roll my shoulders. I try not to look at Cole, since I'm humiliated as it is, so I stand there, hands on my hips, and stare into the trees, hoping he'll forget about what he's seen and leave me be. The smell of pine fills my senses, and I take deep breaths to calm my sick stomach.

"Hey." Cole's hand touches my back and he slides his arm around me. "I'm sorry. I pushed you too hard."

I shake my head and surprise myself when I lean back against him. "No. You didn't. I'm not used to pushing *myself* so hard." A wave of dizziness passes over me, and I grab onto him for support.

His arms tighten around my waist and his breath tickles my ear. "Oh, no you don't. Don't go passing out on me. If you need to, sit down and put your head between your legs."

I steady myself a little. "I'm okay. Just . . . exhausted."

He grabs my arm with his other hand and pulls me against him. I can't help it. I wrap my arms around his waist and lay my head against his chest, listening to his heart beat wildly in my ear. I should pull away because the last thing I want to be doing is hugging someone at the bottom of our biking trail after I've thrown up in the bushes. But I'm too tired to protest.

"You okay now?" He rests his chin on my head and I nod.

And then I realize how disgusting I am. Sweaty and pukey? Not a good combination. I pull back at little, so I can look at him. His eyes are greenish today, the brown flecks lighter in the sunlight. I force myself back into reality and nod. "I think so. I shouldn't have eaten pasta for lunch."

"You ate pasta? No wonder you're sick."

I shrug. "I wasn't planning on training today."

He takes a step back but keeps his hands on my arms. "Next time, I'll call you before we go. Then you'll know not to eat a big meal. I'm sorry." He slides his hands up and down my arms and raises one to push a loose strand of hair out of my eyes. "Your head looks better." He runs a finger just beneath my stupid cut, and my breath catches. His lips are totally calling my name, but then I remember I threw up. Not very romantic. Or hygienic, if we want to get technical.

"Okay." I pull away from him, not wanting him to smell my gross breath and really wishing I had a mint or something. My stomach is still a little uneasy as I put my stuff in his truck, but I'm feeling a lot better now. Besides wanting to curl into a ball and sleep for days. "The good news after all this . . . mess . . ." I gesture toward my bike and the spot where I threw up and look back at him. "My wheels are amazing."

"Just what I wanted to hear." He studies me a second and gives me a smile before putting his gear away. I take off my gloves and stick them in my helmet. As I go to lift my bike in his truck, he grabs it instead. "I'll do it. You get in and relax."

He doesn't have to tell me twice. "Okay." I climb in his truck, and he gets in a few minutes later. He shoots me a smile, and I give him a shaky one back. I lean my head against the seat and close my eyes, loving the air conditioner blowing right in my face. I really hope I don't smell.

"You did awesome out there."

"Not really. Did you not just see what happened?"

"You're not supposed to push yourself to the point of throwing up, but that being said, you really did amazing. My only suggestion is this: don't be afraid to take more risks on your downhill. You're pretty fast, but I saw you hesitate a few times. Don't think about it. Just get in position and keep moving. If you think about it too much, you'll lose time. Or . . . crash."

"I know. Sometimes I see those huge rocks on the trail and freak out a little."

He grabs my hand. "I used to, too." He moves his eyes back on the road and keeps my hand in his.

I don't object.

When we pull into my driveway, my legs feel like Jell-O as I jump down from the truck. I almost fall on my face, but grab the door to steady myself.

Cole comes around and pulls my bike out of his truck before folding his arms and leaning against it. His hazel eyes search mine and I have to wonder what he's thinking. "How about a truth?"

"Right now?" All I want to do is get in a hot shower and into my pajamas. Maybe have someone massage my shoulders. And my feet.

"Yep."

I find myself glancing around. I'm not really sure why. It's not like anyone's even by us. "Okay. I . . . uh . . . hmmm . . ." I wrack my brain for something. Anything that would be interesting about me. "I used to clog."

He raises an eyebrow, and the corner of his mouth raises up, too. "As in, dancing?"

I blush. "Yes. As in dancing."

"What made you quit?"

"I fell in love with biking."

"You clogged until high school?"

I try not to laugh at his shocked expression. "Maybe."

He looks like he's trying not to laugh. "So could you go all 'Lord of the Dance' right here and now?"

"I do have some pretty awesome moves." I do a little jig, sending both of us into a fit of laughter.

"So if you were as awesome of a dancer as you say you were, how did you get into mountain biking?"

I chuckle. "It's kind of embarrassing."

"Oh, I'd love to hear this then."

"I was fifteen and this seventeen-year-old asked me out. I thought I was so cool going out with someone who could drive." He gives me a goofy grin, but I keep talking. "Anyway, he decided to take me mountain biking. He thought he was pretty awesome wearing a bunch of gear and stuff. I just had a helmet and my old ten-speed. And I wore jeans. Nice, right?"

"Hilarious."

"It was. So, he took me to this easy trail in Kaysville and after explaining all the rules to me and talking himself up, I ended up totally smoking him."

"No way!"

I laugh. "I was a little nervous when I first started following him down the trail, because I'd never been before. But then as I made myself pedal faster and flew down the hills, it just clicked and I fell in love. Unfortunately, it wasn't with my date."

"That's the most awesome story ever. That poor kid."

"Yeah. We didn't go out again. I started training myself and saved every penny for a new bike and now, two years later, here I am." I smile, thinking of that first dumb date that turned out to be one of the best days ever. "So, what's a truth from you?"

"A truth from me, huh?" He pushes off the truck and takes a few steps toward me, his eyes not leaving mine. "I'd like to take you out again."

"That's not a truth. That's a fact."

"Same thing."

It's hard, but I make myself look away from his gaze. "When were you thinking?"

"I don't know. How about tonight? If you're feeling up to it after wearing yourself out."

"Sure." I tuck my hair behind my ear. "I'd . . . uh . . . better go get ready."

"Great. I'll pick you up around six."

I stop walking my bike to the garage and turn back. "Oh, what are we doing? So I can dress for the occasion."

He gives me a sly grin. "You'll see."

Not helpful at all.

CHAPTER 26

Mom's waiting for me when I walk inside. She smiles and sets her book down.

"Hey, Emmy."

"Hi." I go to walk past her, but she grabs my hand and pulls me to a stop.

"Could you come sit with me for a minute?"

My heart speeds up. "Sure." I wonder what she's up to. I sit down on the couch, a few inches away.

She searches my face for a moment and smiles. "I haven't talked to you—really talked to you—since we told you what was going on with me. I've tried several times. We both know this."

"I know."

"So, the question is: are you doing okay?"

I shrug. "I'm fine."

"Really? Because it seems to me that you're still avoiding me. And not just me. Everyone. You're not home much anymore, and when you are, you're locked in your room."

"I'm busy."

"With biking. Right."

"Why'd you say it like that?"

She sighs. "Honey, I know you're into biking. I know you love it. But could you at least remember there are people in your family who miss you? I miss you. You won't talk to me. You barely look at me anymore."

I bite my lip.

"I know losing Lucas has been hard. And my diagnosis doesn't help things at all. But right now, I'm okay. Sometimes I have memory lapses, but most of the time I'm fine." She grabs my hand. "I don't want you to push me away, Em. Please. I'm still here. Please stay with me. Don't shut me out."

"I'm not." I really don't want to.

"Honey . . ."

I pull away from her. "I'm fine, Mom. Stop worrying about me." And with that, I go downstairs and lock myself in my room.

Kelsie comes over an hour later, complete with one of her mood lifters.

She pours a bag onto my bedspread. "Nail polish? Check. Chocolate? Check. Chick flick? Check."

"Thanks, Kels."

"So, your mom, right? That's what your emergency text was about?"

I nod. "She wanted to talk to me today. I'm not sure what she wants from me. I'm not ignoring her. I'm keeping myself busy so I don't have to think about her . . . disease."

"It's okay to take some time to think, Em. But don't shut her out forever."

"That's what my mom said." I sigh.

She gives me a nervous smile. "Why don't we start our mini girls' night before Cole gets here? Take our minds off . . . everything."

"What do you want to start with?"

"Nails. What are you wearing tonight?"

"I don't know."

"You look good in blue." She goes in my closet and throws different shirts out. "Try all these on and we'll pick the best one."

"Why can't I just wear . . ." I pull a shirt out from the pile. "This."

Kelsie folds her arms and frowns. "Um . . . no."

"Kels, come on. Just pick something."

"Fine. This one's cute." She holds up a blue T-shirt with ruffles. I'll admit it's pretty cute.

"That's perfect." I take it from her.

She smiles, like she knows she's awesome. "Put it on and let me see what it looks like. Also, where are those jeans I always borrow?"

"Probably at your house."

She thinks about it and finally nods. "Yes. Let's go get them. We can get ready at my house, and I'll bring you back here before Cole gets here."

"Kelsie, is this really necessary? I can just throw something on and—"

"Of course it's necessary!"

I sit back on the bed, defeated.

CHAPTER 27

Cole shows up at my house right on time for our date, of course. And he looks . . . amazing. Jeans, green button-up shirt that brings out his eyes. Hot.

"Uh . . . hi."

"Hey." He smiles as he gets a good look at me. "You ready to go?"

"Yes."

He holds out his arm and leads me to his truck, being a total gentleman, like always.

I raise an eyebrow as I buckle my seatbelt. "Where exactly are we going?"

Cole glances at me out of the corner of his eye. "You'll see. Why don't you relax and enjoy my awesome music."

Rock music blasts through the truck and I pretend to cover my ears. "Oh, come on. Country is way better."

He puts the truck in drive and glances over at me. "Don't swear in my truck, please."

"What are you talking about? I didn't swear."

"Country music is equivalent to a swear word in here."

"Seriously?"

"Do I look like I'm joking?" He's so serious, but there's a playfulness in his eyes. He cracks a smile, making me laugh. "I'm still serious about country music, though. Not a fan. Ever."

"Well, you'll have to get used to it when you ride with me." I push a button on the radio and scroll until I find my favorite station. I sneak a glance at him to see if he's mad, but he sighs and mutters something under his breath. "You're not gonna change it?"

"You're the only one I'd listen to this nonsense for."

I take that as a compliment. "It's not nonsense. It's romantic and fun."

"Half the songs are about someone breaking someone's heart. Or leaving their lover and taking their dog with them."

"No they aren't!" I argue, though I know he has a point.

He chuckles again and we ease into conversation as he drives to wherever our destination is.

It takes me a while, but once Cole starts driving up a dirt road, I realize where we're going.

"Cole . . ." I say as he turns into a dirt parking lot and backs the truck up.

He takes my hand after he parks and meets my eyes. "I thought we could have a nice dinner up here."

"Wow. Bonus points for you, my friend." I smile as I look out onto the valley below. The sun sets in the distance, and I pull out my phone to take a picture. "You're awesome."

"Surprise isn't over." He smiles, opens his door, and jumps down in the dirt. "Hold on a sec. Oh, and don't look in the back no matter what you hear."

He's gone for a little bit, and I know he's doing something in the bed of the truck since the truck keeps moving. Before I know it, he's back. He opens my door and smiles. "My lady."

I roll my eyes as he grabs my hand and helps me out of the truck. He walks me back to the tailgate and my mouth falls open. There are pillows and blankets in the back, and as he reappears, binoculars and a bag of treats.

"The sun is almost set and the stars are amazing up here." He climbs in next to me. "Want to eat now or later?"

"Whenever." He jumps in next to me and hands me a bag. A very familiar bag.

"In-N-Out?"

"Of course."

"I could kiss you right now." As soon as the words leave my mouth, my eyes grow wide and I freeze. "Uh . . . I mean . . ."

Cole glances at my lips, but other than that isn't even phased. "Here's a bottle of water for you. It might be a little warm by now, but it should be okay."

I sneak a look at him as he holds out the water bottle. "Thanks."

He's still watching me, maybe wondering if my little comment was serious or not. Was it? I'm not sure. Maybe. Okay, yes. I really do want to kiss him.

I dig into my burger. "How did I not smell this?"

"I put it in a cooler so you wouldn't."

"Nicely done."

He pops a fry in his mouth. "I know."

I've never really been up here while the sun is setting. It's beautiful. Yellows, oranges, and beautiful shades of red kiss the horizon. I close my eyes for a second, imagining the feel of the wind rushing across my face as I ride my bike down the mountain.

"Wish you were riding right now?"

I open my eyes to find him staring at me. "Always."

"Me too."

I look back at the sun disappearing. "Knowing me, though, I'd run into a tree this late. My eyes aren't the best at night."

"Really?"

"When I don't have my contacts in, I wouldn't be able to tell who's sitting next to me right now."

"That bad?"

I nod. "They're worse at night, even with my contacts in. Especially when I drive. I think I'm a little night-blind."

"Note to self: don't let Emmy drive me around at night."

I chuckle. "Seriously. I scare myself."

We sit in comfortable silence, each finishing our food. "You know, I almost got bit by a rattlesnake up here once."

"Really?"

"Yep. It was right on the edge of the trail. I stopped my bike a few feet away and it started rattling and coiled. I didn't have a choice but to turn around and go back down the trail. It would have bit me if I tried to pass it."

"Holy cow. That's crazy." I search my memory for interesting things that have happened while biking. "A hornet hit my sunglasses once and fell down my shirt while I was

216

riding." I blush as his lips twitch. "It stung me three times before I got it out. It felt like I was on fire."

"You're not allergic, are you?"

"No."

He shivers. "That would have put me in the hospital."

"You're allergic?"

He nods and collects our trash to put back in his cooler. "Since I was a kid. I stepped on a bee when I was five and swelled up like a balloon."

"Oh. That's . . . scary." It's hard to imagine someone being so allergic to something as tiny as a bee.

"Haven't been stung since, but they make me nervous. I have to carry an epinephrine shot with me all the time."

"Yuck. What else don't I know about you?"

He climbs back onto the truck and scoots back to rest against the cab. I follow. "Hmm . . . let's see. I have three sisters and one brother."

"Older or younger? I know about your one sister you told me about. Older, yes?"

"Yes. And so are the rest."

"Oh. So you're the baby?"

"Yep."

"Huh."

He raises an eyebrow. "Why do you say it like that?"

I nudge his shoulder with my own. "Some things make more sense now."

"I have a feeling you're making fun of me."

I laugh. "No, not at all. I'm the youngest, too, so we're twins."

He chuckles again, and before I know it, his arm is around my shoulders.

"Your turn. Tell me something else I don't know about you."

"A truth?"

"Yep."

"Fine." I cuddle up against him and look up at the stars. "I have trust issues . . ."

I feel him nod next to me. "That's a shocker."

I should feel offended, but I'm not. "I'm getting better. I'm sitting here with you, aren't I?"

"True."

"So, one more from you."

"You want to hear another one from me? I'm really not that interesting." He unwraps his arm and grabs my hand. His grip is always so strong. Confident that I won't pull away.

"Sure you are. I like to hang out with you, so that says something."

"You don't hang out with boring people?"

"Not usually."

He laughs. "Okay. A truth."

"And a real one. Not some stupid one like . . . what food you hate the most."

He touches the tip of my nose. "Pickles, if you were wondering."

"Pickles?" I love pickles. Like, love love them. Especially the big crunchy ones. Yum.

"They stink," he adds as he wrinkles his nose.

"You don't know what you're missing. If they had pickle ChapStick, I'd totally use it."

"I wouldn't come near you then."

I go to shove him, but he holds me in place instead. I relax against him. It's nice being so close to someone. He's quiet for a moment and then he drums his fingers on my shoulder. "I've got a good one I think."

"Let's hear it." I snuggle closer, surprising myself for being so . . . bold, I guess?

"Do you know why I bike?"

Wasn't expecting that. I shake my head. "No." I've never thought about it before. I thought he rode because he loved it.

"I . . ." He swallows. "I've never told anyone this, but you might as well be the first."

"You don't have to tell me. If you don't want to."

"I do. I promised I'd tell you a truth."

"Okay. But only if you're alright with it."

He shifts a little, pulling me closer. My heart thumps harder in my chest. "If I would have to trust anyone, it would be you."

"Thanks." I squeeze his hand. "Really. That means more than you know."

"Good." He takes a deep breath. "Okay. Here goes. My name is Cole Evans, and I'm not close to my family. At all."

"Really? I'm sorry."

"My parents aren't the greatest parents ever. I mean, they provide and all that, but we kind of had to take care of ourselves when we were little. And me, being the youngest, having no one . . . I'm guessing I have the biggest problem with it." He shrugs. "My dad got a new job, so that's why we moved here. He's CEO for a pharmaceutical company. He's never home. My mom works for a magazine, so she's locked up in her office all the time. You know about my sister, and my other siblings moved out right when they turned eighteen. So, I was pretty much alone. When my parents told me we were moving, I kind of freaked out. I had everything I could ever want in California. Friends, the beach, my cousins all live there. Why would we ever want to move to Utah?"

"I can see why you were mad. I love California."

"Right? Anyway, I had sponsors looking at my riding there and when we moved . . ." He shakes his head. "It was a rough few months. I still miss my friends. I miss my aunt and uncle. Mia and Madison's parents. They were like *real* parents to me."

"I'm sorry."

"Don't be." He pulls me closer. "I'm doing fine now. It was just hard for a while. And if I wouldn't have moved, I wouldn't have met you."

"Were you wild in California? You seem like a wild child."

He laughs. "A wild child?" He grins. "I guess you could call me that. I wasn't wild with the ladies, but I did do some stupid stuff."

"Like?"

"I broke my ankle long boarding, which I knew before I did the trick that it would probably happen. Did it anyway. Um . . . I drank a little. Got arrested once. Maybe twice."

"You mean to tell me I've been hanging out with a criminal?"

"I've cleaned up my act. Obviously. I was just rebelling to piss off my parents. Or to see if they cared. Which, they didn't. Not really." He shakes his head. "Anyway. Enough about me. Let's hear about you."

"Okay." I think about Mom. She's one of the truths I've never told him, but now that he's shared something so personal with me, I feel like I should share something with him as well. So, I do. "I have a bad habit of holding in my emotions."

"No . . ." He drags it out like he totally knows what I'm talking about.

"Ha. Ha. Very funny. Anyway. I kind of bottle them up forever and they end up exploding every now and then."

"You're not going to explode now, are you?"

"No. You're safe."

"Phew."

"Anyway. I've never been good at talking about things like my feelings with anyone but my family. But lately, I haven't been very good about talking to them either."

"Why? I assumed you guys were close. From what I've seen and heard."

"We are. But . . ." I close my eyes and take a shaky breath. "We found out about a month ago that my mom has early Alzheimer's."

"Really? How old is she?"

"42."

"That's so young. I'm so sorry." He kisses the top of my head, and I try to control my breathing.

"I know. I wasn't expecting it, obviously. None of us were. Especially me and Gavin." I sigh. "They kept it from us for six months."

"Really?"

"I get why they did. They didn't want us to worry until they knew more about it, but still. I was so mad. Still am. Why would you keep something like that from people you love? They should have told us the second they found out. It's not fair."

"Sometimes keeping the truth from others is the only way to deal with hard things. I never tell anyone about my parents because I don't want them to know my weaknesses. Not having support at home. If they did, I'd feel more vulnerable in front of people. Maybe she didn't want you to look for the signs. Everyone forgets things once in a while, so she probably wanted to hide it until she forgot obvious things. It's the same with you bottling up your emotions because you don't want to burden people with your problems. Right?"

That makes so much more sense to me. Why didn't I think of it that way? "Huh."

"Are you doing okay with it? Obviously you're not, since you said you're not really talking to them a lot."

"I'm trying. Admittedly not very hard, though. I felt betrayed and angry at first. Then I wanted to forget about it and pretend nothing was wrong. And now? I'm terrified she's going to forget about me."

"She wouldn't do that."

"It's a neurological disease, Cole. It's going to happen whether she likes it or not. It's just a matter of time."

"Don't they have meds for this kind of stuff? To slow it down?"

I shrug. "I haven't really asked what the medicine does."

"Maybe you should."

"Probably. The whole thing stresses me out. I don't know how to ask, mainly because I don't want to know when she'll start forgetting me."

"She might not ever forget you, Em." He shifts a little and tilts my chin up so I'm looking at him. "You'd be very hard to forget."

His eyes search mine and my stomach flips and skips and does a little jig. I smile and turn away. "That's not true, but thanks. And thank you for bringing me here. You always surprise me. And honestly, I never thought I'd be . . . you know . . . hanging out with you so much."

"Because I'm a womanizer, right? Or player? One-night stand kind of guy?"

I glance over to make sure he's joking. From the smile I see, I know he is. "Something like that."

He chuckles. "Truth time."

"Another one? We've told like five truths tonight. I think that's a record."

"You asked for it."

"Let's hear it then."

"Contrary to what you think, I'm not a womanizer. If you haven't figured it out by now."

"I never said those exact words."

"You implied."

I shrug.

"I've only kissed two girls. And trust me when I say, I sort of regret those kisses now."

"I've been kissed once."

He shifts lower so his face is at my level of shortness and grins. "Do I know this person?" His face is in shadow from the darkness of the night, but as my eyes adjust on his features, I can't help but get lost in those eyes of his. It takes me a second to answer since staring at him makes me lose my train of thought.

"Maybe." *Please don't guess. Please don't guess. It was a one-time thing at a stupid party because of a stupid dare.*

"Hmmm . . ." He reaches over and brushes a strand of hair away from my face. "Who could this person be?"

"I'll never tell." If he knew I've kissed Mark, I'd never hear the end of it. I have to wonder if Mark has already told him though. They *are* on the same biking team after all. Maybe not.

"I bet I can get it out of you. Maybe not right now, but one of these days."

"Never. It's a secret I'll take it to my grave."

He chuckles and continues to stare at me. My body shakes slightly, and it's not from the cold. The way he's looking at me makes my heart beat faster and sends chills through my body. Good chills. He studies my reaction as he runs his fingers along my jaw and into my hair. I lean closer, my eyes closing as his lips touch mine, a whisper of a kiss. He moves closer, his lips gentle but firm as I wrap my arms around his neck.

Kissing him makes me realize I've waited for this moment forever. Cole is everything I want in a guy.

I think of Lucas, then. I never kissed Lucas. And who knows if I really was in love with him. I definitely loved him, but . . .

With that thought, I pull away, giving him a small smile before I sit up. He looks disappointed as he joins me, but doesn't say anything.

"We'd better go. It's getting late," I say.

"You're right. I'll start cleaning things up." He gathers the pillows and treats and jumps off the tailgate to put them away. I hand him the blanket wrapped around me, but he shakes his head. "It's chilly. You can keep it for now."

"Okay." I pull it tight around me as he cleans up everything else. It only takes a moment before he comes back and leans on the tailgate, staring at me.

"You ready?"

I nod and scoot myself to the edge of the tailgate. He helps me down and walks me to the passenger door. I should say something. I need to say something, but my mind won't cooperate. So I stand there and go through the motions of climbing in the truck, shutting the door, and buckling.

The ride home is silent, save for the radio playing softly in the background. He doesn't reach for my hand, doesn't say anything, and avoids my eyes when I look over at him.

Why do I always have to screw everything up?

We make it back to my house pretty fast. He opens my door to help me out and I smile at him when my feet touch the ground. He shuts the door, but instead of walking me to the porch, he leans against the truck with his arms folded. His gaze meets mine and all these different feelings hit me at once, almost knocking me breathless.

"What?" I ask as he stares at me.

"Just thinking."

"You can tell me. You look like you want to."

He shrugs. "Maybe I do."

"Then say it." I think about taking it back. Maybe I don't want to know what he's thinking. But the truth is, I want to know everything he's thinking.

He takes a step closer, his eyes on mine. "Something's been on my mind lately."

"Okay?" Oh, no.

"What are we?"

"What do you mean?" Here it comes. The conversation I've been dreading. I can't handle this. Not now. How do I tell him I don't know what I'm feeling? That I need more time to figure out my jumbled thoughts. My broken, but healing heart.

"Me and you. I . . ." He lets out a frustrated breath. "In the truck . . . Didn't that mean anything to you?"

I hesitate, choosing my words carefully. It meant so much. Too much. But I can't tell him that. I don't want him to waste his time on someone who can't be everything he wants and needs right now. So I lie. "We're friends." I clear my throat. "I don't know how to be anything else."

He laughs, but I can tell it's fake. "Friends. That's all you see us as?"

I swallow and nod. "Of course."

Another step closer. My heart beats a little faster. "I don't think I agree."

"Why not?"

"I don't see you as a friend, Emmy. Friends talk and make jokes. Hang out all the time. But every time I'm with you . . . the only thing I want to do is kiss you. And after taking the chance tonight, I really want to do it again."

The breath whooshes out of my lungs and my heart hammers in my chest as he takes another step closer. I wish I could run. Run in the house and not look back, but I can't. There's something in his expression. The way he's staring at me with those big, hazel, gorgeous eyes that makes me freeze in place. I couldn't run away even if I wanted to.

"Cole . . ." I start.

He's inches away now. He reaches down and tucks a strand of hair behind my ear. "Don't tell me you have to go clean your house or something right now. It would totally kill the moment."

I chuckle. "No. I wasn't going to say that."

"Good." His other hand touches my cheek, and I shiver.

"Cole," I whisper.

"Yes?"

"I don't know what to do."

"About what?"

"About us."

He leans in and panic bubbles in my chest. His lips are so close. So close I could lean in and touch them again with my own. And as much as I want to fight the feeling, I can't. "Emmy. I know you can feel whatever is going on between us. And I know you loved Lucas. But at least let me try. Let me try to be the person you want to be with."

I shiver. "Okay."

"What?" He pulls back a little, his eyes finding mine.

"I said okay." I smile, my cheeks heating.

He touches his forehead to mine. "Really?" I can hear the smile in his voice before he slides a hand to my cheek and kisses me again. Soft, but enough to make me almost melt. "Thank you."

"For what?"

"For letting me in. Even if it's just a little. I care too much about you to let you walk away now." He leans in again and, as his lips touch mine, I slowly wrap my arms around his neck, all thoughts of my broken heart gone.

CHAPTER 28

Kelsie squeals again and dances around my room. "You have got to be kidding me!"

I blush and try not to spill nail polish on my bedspread. "Nope. Not kidding."

"So, is he, you know. An amazing kisser?"

"Yes. Not that I have a lot of experience, but . . . uh . . . it was nice."

She sighs. "I knew it."

"How can you know someone's going to be a good kisser?"

"Have you looked at him lately? That's how you know."

I chuckle and twist the nail polish lid back on before setting it on my night stand. I admire my blue toes and grab a few flower decals to stick on. "Remember when we first met?"

"Ugh. Don't remind me."

"Cute new girl runs into tetherball pole as the whole sixth grade looks on."

"Blood was everywhere. Oh, the memories. I was such a nerd."

"There were so many boys who would have happily taken you to the office. But I was the lucky one who you picked." I smile. "I was so happy I got to miss class for an hour to sit with you."

"I'm glad my pain made you happy." She grins and grabs some purple polish. "And I'm glad you were there. We were meant to be besties. You know that, right?"

"Of course." I really don't know what I'd do without her. Life would be a lot more boring.

"I never got as close to Oakley. Even when all three of us hung out. She was always kind of distant."

"Worried about Lucas, I'm sure."

"Yeah." She's thoughtful as she finishes painting her toenails. "So, when are you and Cole going out again?"

"He's taking me riding today. The Back Country race is next week, so we're gonna train every other day until it's here."

"You'll do awesome."

"Maybe."

"How's your mom?"

"No idea."

"Still haven't talked to her?"

I shake my head. "No."

"Sorry."

"It's fine. I don't know how to talk to her anymore. Which is stupid. Nothing's really changed yet. I'm just . . ."

"Scared."

"Yeah."

"Understandable." She blows on her toes for a second before reaching toward the desk. "Hand me those decals?"

I throw the pack over to her.

"Holy cuteness." She sticks a few on her toes and wiggles them to show me. "We're totally cute."

"For sure."

A song comes on my iPod then and Kelsie's eyes light up. She jumps off the bed and turns it up, blasting it through my room. "I love this song!"

Kelsie's good at everything, but the thing she excels at is dancing. And she's definitely getting her groove on. I would join her, but if anyone saw me dance, they'd tell me to stop trying and sit down. Besides my clogging, I can't dance. Especially hip-hop and stuff. My body doesn't move like that.

So I sit and watch.

And laugh. A lot.

While Kelsie's jamming out, Gavin pokes his head in my room. And you know in the movies when the music suddenly stops playing when something embarrassing happens and all eyes find the person being embarrassed?

Totally happened.

The song ends, and Kelsie is standing in a very interesting pose as Gavin watches from the doorway. Her eyes widen as she meets his gaze, and her face turns bright red. But she doesn't miss a beat. Another song starts playing and she grabs Gavin's hand. "Come jam with us," she says, laughing.

"I was just coming to see what all the commotion was about. And if you ask Emmy, I don't dance."

"You do now," she yells as she twirls around the room.

Leave it to Kelsie to not care what other people think of her.

I wish I could be like that.

Gavin shoots me a helpless look before she starts teaching him how to swing dance.

As I watch them twist their arms around each other, laughing and making fun of each other, I realize something:

They'd be perfect for one another.

CHAPTER 29

Sweat trickles down my neck as I push myself harder up the hill. I can feel Cole's eyes on me, watching, waiting for me to slow down, but I refuse. I keep moving, making sure I'm in the right gear, and when I make it to the top, I let out a whoop, stop my bike, and throw my hands in the air.

"That was awesome," Cole says, sliding his bike to a stop next to mine. "You beat your time and had some time to spare."

I roll my shoulders and take a swig of water. "I did it, huh?" I glance at the GPS on his bike and smile, pumping my fist in the air again. "Yes!"

Cole chuckles. "You did great." He takes a drink as well. "Let's see how you do on the way back down." He squirts some water down his neck and rests his arms on his hand bars for a second, his eyes searching my face.

I feel the blush creep to my cheeks, but I can't look away.

"It's hot," he says, wiping the sweat from his forehead.

Yep. Sweat and all. He's hot.

"You okay?" he asks, a smile creeping to his lips.

"Uh . . . yes. Yep. Everything's perfect."

"Really?" He sits up straight and rolls his shoulders. "You ready to ride back down?"

"Bring it." I turn my bike around and look down the trail. A man walking his dog passes us, gives us a little wave, and keeps moving. Sometimes it's hard riding fast when you know people are running and hiking on the trail.

Even though it says at the bottom Biking Only. People don't pay attention to that "tiny" detail.

But even so, everyone's always so nice in the mountains. I'm not sure why. Maybe because it's peaceful up here.

"You ready?"

Cole pulls me out of my weird train of thought, and I nod. "Yep."

"Okay. Remember, you're allowed to take risks, but don't be stupid."

I sigh. "I know."

He laughs. "Just making sure you know that."

"See you at the bottom." I clip my pedals in and head down the trail.

A bug hits my glasses, but luckily it doesn't splatter. I keep moving, avoiding a few people along the way. I slide my bike around a sharp turn and brake so I don't fly off the edge, then keep moving.

I maneuver around an old rotted log, hit a pretty big rock while doing so, but stay upright. I'm getting better at keeping my bike in control. Which is good.

Dirt flies on either side of me, and as I zoom through a puddle, mud splatters onto my legs. And up my back. I can feel it soaking through my shirt and I'm sure it's caked onto my spandex.

Oh well.

Faster. Faster. The wind rushes across my face, making my adrenaline pump even harder. A steep hill is up ahead and I shift into fourth, fifth, and finally sixth gear as I approach. I go a little slower, but not much, stand up, lean back, and keep my hands on my back brake. I know from experience to keep my hand off the front brake. If I pull it by accident, I'll flip over my handlebars again.

Not going to happen today. I don't want to get stitches again, especially since I got them out only a few days ago.

Once I make it down that hill, I push myself all the way to the bottom, passing a few bikers going up.

I duck under a low-hanging tree branch and almost hug the side of a rocky ledge as I go around a group of bikers heading up.

I can see the parking lot through the trees, so I pedal faster until the trees are behind me, and I let the dust settle as I come to a stop.

Cole joins me seconds after I make it down and pumps a fist in the air. "That was awesome!"

"I know, right? I did so much better than I usually do." I pull out my water again and take a drink as I sit on my bike.

"You hit that mud puddle, too?"

I try to glance behind me at my butt, but can't really see if there's mud there. It's all over my bare legs though. "Yep."

Cole wipes some off of his own leg and reaches over to smear a little on my cheek.

"What was that for?" I say, wiping it off.

"I thought you'd look cute with a little dirt on your face."

I get a small splatter of mud off my shin and rub it along his jaw, feeling a little bit of stubble there. I smile at my handiwork as Cole sits there, not even attempting to get away. After a second, he grabs my hand and leans over, still on his bike, and kisses me right in front of whoever's watching.

If anyone's watching.

And for once I don't care. I kiss him back, reveling in the adrenaline I still feel and the fact that I have a boyfriend who loves biking as much as I do.

I have a boyfriend.

Me.

I'm not sure what to do with myself. Or that knowledge.

CHAPTER 30

A week later, after intense training with Cole, Mom finds me in my room. She doesn't knock, but stands in my doorway until I look up.

"Hey," I say. "Everything okay?"

She nods. "Just seeing how you're doing."

I set my racing clothes out on the bed and smooth out my jersey. I've always loved this jersey. Orange and white. Reminds me of an orange creamsicle. Which sounds really good right now. I wonder if we have any.

"You have a race tomorrow?"

I look up at her, noticing her pale skin and loose hair falling from her bun. "Yep. Tomorrow morning."

"Oh. You ready for it?"

"I think so." I look at the bottom of my shoes and make sure there's not dirt stuck in my clips. I want them perfect. I won't have any blemishes or mistakes tomorrow morning that could make me lose.

"What time's it at?"

"Nine."

"Where?"

"Ogden."

She's quiet for a moment as I dust off my dirty gloves. "Cool."

She continues to stand there and watch as I get my stuff ready. I glance at her a few times, hoping she's not having one of her . . . episodes. But she looks fine. Normal. Maybe even a little sad.

"I hope you do okay tomorrow."

"Me too."

"Is anyone taking you or are you going by yourself?"

"Kelsie and Cole are coming with me."

"I still have to meet this Cole."

I hesitate. "I know."

I wait for her to tell me to be careful with boys. That they're only after one thing, but she doesn't. She stares at me a moment longer and sighs. "Be safe tomorrow, okay?"

"Okay." I stand up and we stare at each other for a moment before she turns around and heads back up the stairs.

I used to be so close to Mom. I don't know how I've managed to push her so far away. It's my fault. I know it. My fault because I'm scared to admit she has a problem. Still. Maybe after my race tomorrow, I'll talk to her about it. I'm getting used to the idea that she's not going to get better. That she'll be a totally different person in the near future. Maybe I'll be okay with it. Maybe it's not as bad as I think it's going to be.

Or not.

I really don't know.

Yes. I'll talk to her tomorrow. I don't want anything to bring me down from this high I've had from training every day.

Everything else is perfect right now. Perfect and amazing. And I want it to stay that way.

CHAPTER 31

Back Country. The one day I've been training for, for weeks. It's finally here. The day I'm going to beat Whitney.

Or *maybe* beat her.

Hopefully.

As I slide my gloves on, I can't keep the negative voice taking over in my head.

You're not good enough. You can't do this. She's so much better than you are.

I tell it to shut up. I have to calm my nerves and figure out what the heck I'm supposed to do to win.

Butterflies occupy the space of my stomach and I take deep breaths before lining up at the starting line. It's a cross country race. A bunch of downhill and lots of climbing is involved, too. I can do this. Breathe and I'll be okay.

I see Kelsie standing behind the finish line and give her a little wave. She waves back, her phone raised, probably taking a zillion pictures of me. I'm so happy she's here. She's always here when I need her.

The boys race right after us. I glance at Cole, who's over with the guys getting ready. He smiles, his eyes meeting mine, and puts his fingers to his lips.

I do the same back to him and he smiles and turns back around.

"Don't even tell me. You and Cole now?" Whitney's voice grates on my ears, and I try to tune her out. I don't want her to mess me up. Even before the race.

Keeping my eyes on Cole, I say, "Do you have a problem with that?"

She laughs. "He's just so much better than you. I don't know why he bothers."

I ignore her, fuming, and focus on putting my gloves on. I flex my fingers, making sure they're snug. I check my brakes, my gears, everything once again, even though I've already checked them a dozen times already. It gives me something to do instead of letting my nerves get the best of me.

"Riders get ready."

I shake off my nerves and climb on my bike, clip my shoes into the pedals, and get ready. Focus. Breathe. I've got this. Five miles of hard riding and I'll be done. Keep it together. Remember what Cole taught me.

The gunshot goes off and the race starts.

Whitney shoots to the front of the line, and I keep a good pace in third, behind Whitney and a girl in blue with dark hair. By the way she's riding, she knows what she's doing. I've got my work cut out for me today.

Dirt from the trail picks up around the riders, and I'm thankful I have my sunglasses on. I duck under a low-hanging tree branch and follow the bikers ahead of me down the narrow part of the trail. One side is a bunch of trees and a twenty-foot drop off, the other side is solid rock.

I ignore the small part of me that's afraid of heights and focus on the back of the girl in front of me, keeping calm, even breaths.

The first part of the race is easy—mostly just turns and dirt on a smooth surface.

Then the hills come. I'm ready. I shift gears before the first hill and charge on up. The trail widens a tad, but not enough, so I keep my position and wait.

The sun beats down on my white and orange jersey, and I feel the sweat bead on my forehead. If I can keep up with Cole, I can keep up with these girls. I glance ahead and pump my legs harder. Still third and time to move up. I look down at my GPS. I've ridden about three miles now.

The trail widens as the trees thin and nothing but weeds and sagebrush take up both sides of the trail. I suppress a grin as I pass the second-place rider and push myself until I'm right behind Whitney's pink spandex. She's fast, but I match her pace, staying far enough away, but close enough. I'd pass her, but the trail has thinned again and I don't want to get pushed into the weeds by moving too early.

Playing it safe, I keep up behind her, silently thanking Cole for helping me get my endurance up.

My butt is killing me by the time we make it to the last climb. Switching gears again, I start up the hill, avoiding big rocks that could throw the entire race. The back of my shirt is sticky with sweat, and my legs feel like they're on fire, but I keep going, noting when Whitney slows just a tad. The trail widens enough for two bikes, and I take a chance, pushing myself as hard as my body will allow. We reach the top, neck and neck, and I look ahead at the last downhill before the finish line.

It's completely covered in rocks.

Cole said risks were okay to take, as long as I'm not stupid, so I speed up, shift into sixth gear, and stand, leaning back behind my seat as I navigate over the rocks. I'm thankful I have a shock, because my bike would be bouncing out of control if I didn't.

I reach the bottom and have no idea where Whitney is. People are cheering. I push myself harder than I've ever pushed before in a race, and when I cross the finish line, my eyes fill with tears when I see Whitney is two seconds behind me.

I did it. I won!

Cole reaches me first, ripping me off my bike and squishing me in a huge bear hug. I laugh and cough and cry all at the same time. "You did it, Em!"

"I know!" I hug him back as he spins me around, not setting me down until Kelsie races over. She tackles me and, seeing how wobbly my legs are, we both fall into a heap in the dirt. I sit there, tears running down my dirty cheeks, and don't even bother trying to get up.

"You were amazing, Emmy!"

I laugh and wipe happy tears away. "Thank you. I can't believe I did it."

I look up as someone reaches a hand down to help me up. Whitney. "Good race, Emmy. See you next month." She gives me a tiny smile and walks away, head held high.

"Wow. That was . . . nice," I say, staring after her.

"I told you. She may not be as bad as you think," Cole says with a wink.

Kelsie grabs my hand. "Let's go claim your prize. I think it's like $100 or something." She bounces on her toes. "Oh, and by the way, your brother's here."

"Gavin's here?"

She points to him coming out of the crowd as he rushes over to me and wraps me in a hug. "You did it, Em! That was seriously crazy."

"I didn't even know you were here." I squeeze him back, hard. He's never come to one of my races before. I'm so happy to see him. "Is Mom or Dad here, too?"

He shakes his head. "No. But Mom wanted to come. She even got in the car with me, but Dad made her stay home. She wasn't feeling very well."

"What's wrong with her?"

"She thinks she's getting the flu. Dad was kind of worried about her so he made her go to bed and told me to tell you they'll make it to your next one."

"Oh." My mood dampens and I frown. I didn't realize how much I wanted them to come until this moment. "So, how long have you been here? Did you see the whole race?"

He nods. "I snuck in right before you started. I've never seen you race before, and I knew this was a big deal for you."

"Thanks, Gav." I hug him and pull away, finding Cole's hand again. I don't miss the look Gavin gives me, but it's not a bad one. Just one that I'm sure means he'll embarrass me later.

Someone calls the boys group to go line up and I give Cole a smile. "You're racing next. Get over there and I'll see you when you're finished."

"Yes, ma'am." He winks and leaves us alone.

CHAPTER 32

The day passes in a blur. Cole has two races, so we spend most of the day at the trail. The high of winning the race is addicting. I'm not sure what I want to do when we're done here, but I know it will involve Cole.

Kelsie hugs me again. "I'm so proud of you, Em. You were amazing."

"Thanks."

As we watch the end of Cole's second race, which of course he wins, we wait for him to get his winner's check and medal. After everyone claps and takes pictures, he walks over and brings someone with him.

It's an older guy, maybe in his thirties. He's grinning as Cole stops in front of us. "Emmy, this is Daniel. My sponsor. He'd like to talk to you for a second."

Daniel reaches out his hand to me and squeezes it tight as he shakes it. "I saw you race, Emmy. You did awesome. I was wondering if you'd like to discuss a possible sponsorship with Edge. I'd like to see you race next month, and we could do dinner after, depending on your outcome."

"That sounds . . . amazing."

He smiles. "Perfect." He hits Cole's shoulder and then shakes his hand. "See you, bro. Great race today."

"Thanks, Daniel."

We watch him walk away and Cole grins at me.

"A sponsor?" It's all I can say. I never dreamed this would happen. Even if it's just dinner next month. A sponsor was actually talking to me. To me. "You didn't have to tell him about me."

"You earned it. And besides, he saw the race. He saw how good you rode. I had nothing to do with it."

"You brought him here, though." I nudge him with my shoulder and he chuckles.

"I may have had a little to do with it, but only a little." He pulls me to him, and I put my hands on his chest as he gives me a wicked grin. "I'm proud of you." He kisses me, and I have to hang on to him to support my legs which are starting to ache from my race.

"Seriously? In front of everyone?"

I glance at Kelsie. "You're one to talk." She always kisses whoever she was dating in front of people. Didn't matter where they were. The back seat of my car, in front of her locker at school. Sometimes *in* her locker making out. No exaggeration.

"I know." She grins.

Cole slips his hand through mine. "You want to get out of here? I haven't really eaten all day."

"Yes. We can go grab a shake, too. Sound good?"

"That sounds great." I pull Gavin over. "Hey. Want to come get a shake with us?"

"Sure. I can drive if you want."

"Let me lock my bike up on my car. Can you drop me off back here after?"

"Of course."

After locking up our bikes, we follow Gavin to his car. "Shotgun!" Kelsie yells.

I happily let her take it since I'm looking forward to sharing the back seat with Cole. Not that we'll do anything; I just feel like being close to him.

We all pile inside and head down the road.

"Where are we headed?" he asks, glancing back at us.

"Wherever. Are you guys hungry for shakes or food, too?"

"I'm starving," Cole says, slipping his arm around my shoulders.

"Me too," I admit. "How about Wendy's?"

A collective yes echoes through the car.

Kelsie turns the radio up, and we all jam out to the song blasting through the speakers.

Gavin stops at a four-way stop, tapping his hands on the steering wheel. Cole moves his arm for a second to adjust his seatbelt and everything seems perfect.

I glance out the window at the setting sun. It was a perfect day. The perfect day to win a race.

Gavin pulls forward then, and no one else sees the car zooming through the stop sign until it's too late.

Everything is in slow motion.

The sound of screeching metal, shattering glass, and screams fill the air. I don't know who's screaming, but it pierces my ears and leaves a ringing there until everything goes still.

Pain radiates through my entire body, especially my neck. I try to move, but can't. My eyes can't focus and I can't get a good breath.

"Cole?" I gasp, trying to take in another breath. My lungs won't cooperate. They feel like fire, burning me from the inside out. I close my eyes from the pain and focus on breathing in and out as tears stream down my cheeks.

"I'm here, Emmy. Stay with me, okay?"

"I . . ." My voice trails off. It hurts to talk. To breathe. To move. Everything hurts. "Can't . . . breathe . . ." I try to suck in another breath, and it hurts so bad I think I might pass out.

Sirens wail in the distance and I try to focus on those. Anything that will stop the pain.

They're getting closer. Help is coming. We're going to be okay.

"Emmy," Cole says, again. Louder and more worried.

He says it again and again. I can't see him. All I hear is his frantic voice, and I can feel his fingers on my face, in my hair.

That's the only thing I can hold on to when the darkness overtakes me.

CHAPTER 33

I'm here and then I'm there, slipping in and out of consciousness. My mind is all over the place, but my body is stuck in Gavin's smashed car.

I hear Gavin calling my name this time. Again and again. I strain to open my eyes and see his face. He's standing outside, leaning in what's left of my window. Blood trails down his cheek, and his hands are covered in it, as well. I wonder if it's his blood or mine.

He's saying something, but I can't understand him as black dots fill my vision again. He doesn't reach inside. Doesn't touch me. I want him to touch me. To tell me I'm going to be okay. That it's only my imagination that I can't feel anything below my waist.

I can't breathe.

"Paramedics are here. You're going to be okay. They're going to get you out of there."

I might be imagining it, but he looks like he's crying. Tears trail down his cheeks and he doesn't bother wiping them away.

My brother's crying? Why? I'm right here. I'm alive. Or am I? I can't feel my body anymore. It's like I'm floating. Weightless.

Sitting in my haze, a familiar face keeps filling my thoughts. The person I need most right now. The one who would hold me and tell me I'm going to be okay.

Mom.

I want my mom.

I never told her how much I love her. How sorry I am for staying away.

What if I die, and she'll only remember a hateful teenager who wasn't grateful for anything she did? What if I never get the chance to tell her how much she means to me? How afraid I am that she'll forget me.

Flashing lights reach the corner of my eye, and I feel myself slipping again.

My breathing is ragged. It hurts so much. I just want the pain to stop.

Fingers find mine and someone squeezes my hand.

It's Cole. I know it is. I can't turn my head, but I can feel the familiar touch of his hand. The way his fingers intertwine with mine. He's here. He's trying to keep me safe. Letting me know he's near.

I don't know how long it takes, but the paramedics finally get me out of the car and strap me to a board. I see Cole trying to get to me. He's hurt. I see the gash on his cheek and smaller cuts pepper his perfect face.

He's only there a moment and then he's gone.

I don't know where Kelsie is. Or Gavin.

Gavin.

Where's Gavin?

My chest hurts. With every breath, it feels like someone is stabbing me with a knife. Tears slip down my cheeks and wet my hair as they settle in my scalp.

Voices enter my consciousness and I try to make sense of what they're saying.

"Collapsed lung . . . spinal cord . . . stitches . . ." They blur together after that.

The ambulance ride is a blur. I try to move, but can't. Everything's foggy. I try to suck in a breath again, but my lungs feel weighed down by something.

"It's okay, Emmy. We're almost to the hospital," says a voice I don't recognize.

Where's Gavin?

I picture him bleeding on the side of the road. No one able to help him. But then I remember the car hit my side. My door. He's probably fine.

The ambulance stops, and I'm wheeled out on a stretcher and rushed into the emergency room.

More faces. I don't recognize any except the paramedic from the ambulance.

Everyone is calm, but the panicked expressions in their eyes when they look me over give them away.

I want Mom.

They ask me questions, but my brain isn't working. All I can do is lay and watch as they put a needle in my arm. I don't even feel it.

My breathing isn't getting any better, and before I know what's happening, a doctor shoves a needle into my chest. It's attached to a tube. The pain is so intense that I scream. It echoes off the white walls and the nurses try to calm me down as I try to get away from them. Anything to get rid of the pain.

"It's okay, Emmy," someone says.

A strange feeling rushes through me as the meds kick in.

The last thing I see is doctors and nurses with masks waiting for me to fall asleep.

CHAPTER 34

The white hallway seems to go on forever as I walk, a piece of paper tight in my hand. I pass a nurse's station, an elevator, and plenty of rooms, but I don't stop until I reach room 205.

I stand outside to put my emotions in check. Thoughts of what I'm going to say swirl around my mind, and I take a breath to prepare myself before I open the door. My hand seems to raise on its own and I knock.

Several beats later, the door opens.

Lucas's mother stares back at me, her face drawn, haggard, and lacking sleep. "Emmy." She smiles. "Come in. He's been waiting for you." She gestures around the curtain, blocking the room from view. "I'm going to get some lunch, so I'll be back in a little bit."

The door shuts behind her and I stand on the other side of the curtain, getting myself ready to see him.

"Emmy?"

Lucas's voice drifts toward me and I only hesitate a second before I push past the curtain.

I know I'm dreaming, but the sight of him still makes my stomach drop.

He looks so different. An IV pumps into his hand. It looks like a child's hand. Small, bony, and pale. He's so pale. I don't know what to say, so I take a seat near his bed, trying to avoid looking too close at him. I don't want to remember him this way. So . . . fragile.

He reaches his hand out to take mine, and I look up at him. He may look sick and miserable, but his eyes are blue, bright, and alive. "Thanks for coming," he says. "Hopefully none of the nurses gave you a hard time."

"Why would they do that?"

He shrugs. "They can't keep their hands off me." He chuckles and squeezes my hand.

"Oh." I gaze at his frail body. Even though he looks so different, like half of himself disappeared, he's still Lucas. My Lucas. The boy I've been in love with for years. He's still the same. Still trying to make me laugh. I think about all we've been through. The late-night talks in his back-yard, the drives through the canyon admiring the changing leaves in the fall. The way he talked to me at school, even when he had a girlfriend and never treated me any differently. I can't let that go. I don't want to let him go.

He studies me, his right eyebrow lowering a fraction. "What's wrong, Em? You're too quiet."

"Oh, nothing. I'm okay."

"You sure? You're not in trouble or anything, right? If your parents didn't want you to come, you could have said no."

I shake my head and let out the breath I'm holding. "They told me you wanted to see me. They said . . ." I pause and say the words, even though they almost break me. "You're dying."

"I did want to see you." He gives me a sad smile. "And yes. I'm dying."

It hangs in the air, and I have to tell myself to keep breathing. *In and out. In and out.* I need to stay calm. I knew this was coming, but it still hurts. It's not fair.

"Em," he says.

His voice draws me out of my thoughts, and I jump, making myself focus on him again. "Yeah?"

"I wanted you to come see me one last time. Before . . ." He swallows and shakes his head. "Let's not talk about that right now. The reason I asked you here is because I needed to tell you something."

I glance up, meeting his eyes. "Okay?"

He doesn't skip a beat, just presses on. "I'm in love with you, Emmy."

My heart speeds up, and my breath whooshes out of my lungs. My mouth drops open, and I close it again, not knowing what to say.

He laughs, though it sounds forced. "I've practiced saying that to you for . . . years really. I'm days away from dying, and I wasn't man enough to say it before." He lets go of my hand and reaches up to touch my cheek. "I've loved you since you first moved in next door. All those years ago." His voice catches, and I cover his hand with mine. "I'm sorry I waited so long to tell you."

A tear slips down my cheek, running a trail to our fingers. "I love you, too," I whisper.

I memorize his face, knowing it's probably the last time I'll see him alive. His deep blue eyes are burned into my mind. His smile, teasing and playful—though gone now, I can still see it.

"Take care of my sister for me, okay?"

"Okay," I promise, though I broke it long ago.

He leans back on his pillow, his eyes never leaving mine. "I wish things were different. I wish we had more time." He smiles, his eyes swimming with tears as I hold on to his hand like a lifeline. "That's all I want. More time. To take you on a real date. To hold your hand while we walk down the street together." He sighs as tears prick my eyes. "I'm an idiot for not telling you sooner."

"You're not."

He ignores me and pulls my hand to his lips. "Thank you, Em. For always being there, even when I didn't deserve it." His body fades before my eyes, and I know my memory has come to an end.

Don't go. Please. Not yet.

The room starts to disappear, taking Lucas away from me all over again. I start to panic. I don't want him to leave. I need more time. Time to say all the things I meant to say that day.

But time never stops. It just keeps going and going, not caring who it leaves behind.

And at that moment, I despise it.

CHAPTER 35

There's no way to fix time. To warn yourself about an impending accident. To push the brakes a little bit quicker.

If there was a way to go back, I would. But there isn't. Time just keeps moving slowly forward whether I want it to or not. It's a constant, never-changing thing that will never ever go away no matter how hard you wish it.

My head feels heavy. Like I'm swimming through a suffocating fog. Thoughts of Lucas fill my head, and I try not to cry as I think of the memory I was lost in for a while.

When my eyes finally open, I blink a few times before I notice I'm lying in a hospital room. I blink again and memories of the accident flood my brain.

Then the pain hits, and it takes everything in me not to call the nurses station and ask for more pain meds. I'm sure they've already given me plenty.

The room is pretty dark so I know it's late.

Someone snores quietly to my right, and I try to turn my head, but I can't. It's in a brace or something.

It doesn't matter though; I'd recognize that snore anywhere.

Dad. I don't want to wake him. I'm sure I've put him through enough tonight.

I lift my hand, frowning at the IV in it. I follow the little tube until it reaches the bag of fluid on a pole next to the bed.

Drip. Drip. Drip.

I've never been a fan of needles, and now one's taped to my hand. But honestly, that's the least of my problems.

I take a moment to access my injuries. My chest kills every time I breathe, but it's nothing like the pain in the ambulance. I'm guessing they blew my lung back up, but it still feels like it's on fire. My head hurts. I reach my hand up and feel a bandage near my temple. Stitches again, I'm guessing.

A monitor beeps next to me. I want to move. Change positions. Anything. But as I try to shift and get in a more comfortable position, I remember my legs. They tingle. Like they're asleep and trying to wake up.

I try to wiggle my toes, but fail. My foot. Nothing.

No. *Please.* I can't be paralyzed.

Nothing but tingling.

My eyes water, and I put a hand to my mouth to try to stop the sob that escapes anyway.

Someone's foot hits the floor, and as my eyes adjust to the dark, I see Dad's outline as he comes to my side. He doesn't say a word, just wraps his arms around me and holds me while more sobs wrack my body. The pain from his embrace is easy to ignore.

I can't get a hold of myself.

I don't know how long Dad sits with me. Long enough to soak his shirt and clog my sinuses. He hands me a tissue, and I wipe my eyes and nose. "Are you okay?"

I shake my head as best as I can. *No. I'm not okay. Can't you see I'm never going to be okay again?*

"We're gonna get through this, okay, Bug? You're going to be fine. I promise."

I close my eyes. He shouldn't make promises he can't keep. I can't be positive right now. My whole life has been torn to pieces because of a stupid bike race. If I hadn't won, I wouldn't be here now. I'd be sulking in my bedroom. Letting Cole kiss me to cheer me up. I'd be okay.

"Where's Mom?" My voice is hoarse, and I clear my throat.

"She's home. She'll be here in the morning when you go in for your surgery."

"Surgery?"

"Honey, you have a collapsed lung and a spinal cord injury. They're not sure how serious yet, since the swelling is bad and they can't tell everything, but . . ." He trails off and clears his throat before continuing. "They're going to try and fix it, but these injuries take time to heal."

"I already know it's bad, Dad. I can't move my legs." Tingling. Just tingling.

He sighs and the pain I see on his face makes me want to cry all over again. "I know."

"Will I walk again?"

"They don't know. Like I said. These injuries take time to heal. I don't think . . ." He trails off. "Maybe you should get some sleep. We can talk about this tomorrow."

"I want to know. Tell me."

"Are you sure?"

I ignore the question. "What will the surgery do?"

"I don't know all the details, besides fixing your lung, of course. Once the surgery is over, and you've recovered well enough, we'll start physical therapy."

"So I could walk again? Maybe?"

He squeezes my hand. "Maybe. Sometimes your spinal cord is in shock after you get in an accident like this. If the swelling goes down quickly, they can tell a bit more about how damaged it may be. But it may not be broken at all. Things might be okay. It could go either way, honestly."

I squeeze my eyes shut and tears slide down my cheeks. "I never should have started mountain biking. None of this would have happened."

"Honey. You love biking. Accidents happen. And it wasn't even biking that did this to you. The driver who hit you ran a stop sign. It wasn't your fault or Gavin's at all."

Gavin. "Where is he?"

He hesitates. "He's . . . having a hard time. Mom went home with him. I'm sure he'll be right back here tomorrow."

"Is he okay?"

He nods. "A few stitches, but nothing major."

"Cole and Kelsie?"

"Kelsie has a broken collar bone and Cole has some bumps and bruises, but otherwise, they're fine. It's a miracle you weren't killed."

"I'm glad they're okay."

A miracle I wasn't killed. But what about my legs? They weren't saved. Why did it have to happen to me?

I regret my thoughts as soon as I think them. I wouldn't wish this on anyone else.

My mind wanders to all the things I won't be able to do anymore.

Walking.

Running.

Biking.

I bite my lip to keep from crying again.

"It's okay, Bug. You can cry. It's okay to cry."

"I know," I squeak.

"Bad things happen sometimes. We don't know why, but they do. I know you'll pull through this, and you'll be okay. You're strong."

"I'm not."

"You are."

I stare at the ceiling and don't say anything else. Dad pats my hand and gives it a kiss. "I'll let you get some sleep. You have a big day tomorrow." He moves away, and I hear him get comfortable on the couch again.

"I'm sorry, Daddy."

"Don't you dare be sorry. You didn't do anything wrong."

I know that, but it still hurts. The tears start again and they last until morning.

CHAPTER 36

The anesthesia wears off again, and I blink a few times to get the blurriness out of my vision.

"You okay, honey?"

Mom. She's here, just like Dad said she would be. I glance over as she grabs my hand. She smiles, and tears once again fill my eyes. "Mom. You're here."

"Of course I'm here."

"I thought I'd never get to talk to you again."

She squeezes my hand tight. "And I thought I'd lost you."

I give her half a smile. I don't know what to say. How to act. I almost died in a horrible crash, yet here she sits. She's looking at me like she always has. With love. She knows me. She loves me. She remembers me still.

At that moment, I realize how stupid I've been. Selfish, even. Putting my own needs before hers. Even if I'm still having a hard time wrapping my head around the fact that she has an incurable disease, she's still here. She's still my Mom. And I'm going to live every day like it's the last thing she'll remember. Because that's all I'll have when she's gone. Memories.

I stare at our hands and take a deep breath. I have so much to apologize for. "I'm so sorry, Mom. I'm sorry for everything. I was just so . . . scared. I don't want you to be sick. I don't want you to . . . to forget me." I choke on the last word, and the tears fall freely.

She brushes my hair out of my face. "I'm scared too, Emmy. You have no idea how bad." She wipes a few of her own tears away and hands me a tissue. "But we just keep going. Keep moving and we'll be okay. Both of us."

"I know."

"I want you to know that my mind isn't gone yet. I have little memory lapses, forget stupid things, but my memories are still there. My brain still works. I know who everyone is, I remember things back when you were a baby." She leans forward, her dark eyes bright. "I'm not going to forget you. I promise."

"Don't make promises you can't keep." We both know she won't remember me as the years go by, and I guess I don't have to worry about that for a while. But still. The thought of that day coming fills me with dread.

She frowns, but the tenderness of her expression lets me know how much she means what she says. "I won't forget you. As long as you help me remember, there's no way I could."

"I'll try my hardest."

"Just don't ever avoid me again, okay? I've missed you more than you'll ever know."

"I've missed you, too." I squeeze her hand again. "I love you, Mom."

"Love you, too." She leans forward and kisses me on the forehead. "You just get better, okay? Then we'll talk more. I have a lot to tell you about the medications I'm taking, which are helping so far. And I really want you to come to a doctor's appointment with me. So you can ask questions. Okay?"

"Okay." And I'm serious.

"And don't forget our girls' nights. No blowing me off ever again."

"Never again."

She smiles. "We'll have to do something extra special when you get out of the hospital."

"Deal."

She stands and heads toward the door. "Gavin's been waiting to see you. I'm going to send him in, okay?"

"Okay."

She's gone for a second, and the door opens. Gavin walks in, a butterfly Band-Aid above his left eye. He walks over to the bed and sits down next to me. His eyes are red and swollen, and I have to think really hard to remember the last time I saw him cry. Besides last night.

"Gavin," I say and reach my hand toward him.

He doesn't take my hand, just puts his head in his own hands and starts to sob. "I'm so sorry, Emmy. So, so sorry."

"Gavin, please. It's not your fault."

He wipes at his eyes. "I should have been paying attention. I should have—"

"Someone else ran the stop sign, Gav. It wasn't your fault."

"Still. I was driving. And now look at you. Your legs . . ."

I try to be brave, even though I'm having a hard time convincing myself of it. "I'm going to be fine."

"I'm sorry, Emmy," he says again. He leans forward, grabs my hand, and puts his forehead on my bed. I place my free hand in his hair, and he sobs until he doesn't have any tears left.

CHAPTER 37

When you're in the hospital, the days blur together. They're long and boring and, to be honest, the hospital food sucks.

"Can you feel this?"

I glance at the doctor at the end of my bed. He's putting hot and cold packs on my legs. "Warm."

He nods and smiles. "Great. This?" He set the pack on my shin, and I feel the cold seep through my skin.

"Cold."

His smile widens. "Perfect. Now, can you wiggle your left toes for me?"

I focus on my toes, telling my brain to make them move, and I'm surprised when they do. Barely, but they do. I suck in a breath and raise my hand to cover my mouth. "They moved," I whispered.

He pats my leg. "I believe they did. Can you do your right foot?"

I stare at them and smile as they move back and forth. Not as much as the left, but it's enough to make my heart quicken and my eyes fill with tears.

"Great job, Emmy. You're making great progress already. We'll start physical therapy as soon as we can and get you out of here. Sound good?"

I nod and lay my head back on the pillow. I glance down at my toes again and wiggle them for good measure, which makes me want to smile and cry at the same time. Mostly because I never thought I'd be able to do it again. Wiggle my toes. Something so tiny and simple. I think of how I took the use of my legs for granted every single day before the accident. Never again. I'm going to be more grateful. About everything.

A few hours later, I'm still reeling from the fact that I'm starting to feel things again so soon. Mom and Dad cried, of course, and I'm not gonna lie: I did too.

Cole hasn't been to see me yet, which makes my heart hurt, but Kelsie has. She came the morning after the accident a week ago and has been here almost the entire time since. Right now, she sits on the edge of my bed with ten different colors of nail polish in front of her. She studies my toes as she applies each color with a shaky hand, since her other arm is in a sling, and finally looks at me with a smile. "Rainbow toes," she says as she paints my baby toe red.

"I like them." I try to wiggle them again to admire them, and they move, just a little. I smile.

When I look up, Kelsie's staring at my feet. She hesitates and swallows before meeting my eyes. "I'm so glad you're starting to feel them again. I can't even . . ." she trails off, and I grab her hand as she turns her head away from me.

"I know, Kels. But I'm going to be okay."

She nods, wipes the moisture from her eyes, and shakes her head while clearing her throat. "I'll do your fingernails too if you want." She picks up the blue polish and grabs my hand to set it down in front of her, sliding some polish on my pinky.

"That would be great. I'm so bored here. There's nothing to do."

I glance at the books on the table next to me. I can only read so much without giving myself a headache and having my eyes freak out. But the only way to let my spinal cord heal is to sit still. I can't wait to start physical therapy.

"You heard from him yet?" Kelsie asks.

I know exactly who she's talking about, so I shake my head.

"He won't return my texts either. I wonder if he's okay."

I think of the last time I saw Cole. Just before they put me in the ambulance. He looked so . . . broken.

"I'm sure he is," Kelsie says, though she doesn't look me in the eye.

I miss him and have to wonder why he hasn't come to see me. Maybe he's afraid of what he'll see. Maybe he resents the fact that I might not walk again and doesn't want to deal with it.

I don't know.

"He'll come around," she says. She winces as she moves, her sling for her broken collar bone shifts a little.

"You feeling better?"

She laughs. "Don't worry about me at all. It's just a flesh wound."

I raise my eyebrow. "Not really. It's a broken collar bone. No flesh was injured."

"True. I'm fine though. It's feeling awesome." She gives me a shaky fake smile.

"I'll bet."

"It's crazy. The whole accident. Right?"

I nod as she stares at my toes. "We're lucky to be here," I say.

"I know."

"Have you seen Gavin today?"

She looks up, a blush touching her cheeks. "He was here earlier. I saw him in the lobby."

"Why are you blushing?"

She avoids my eyes, but can't hide her smile. "No reason."

"You like my brother!" I burst out laughing.

Her eyes widen and she almost falls off the bed. "No I don't! Brothers are off limits. Especially when it's your best friend's brother."

I laugh again at her horrified expression. "It's okay, Kelsie. If you two didn't notice each other, I was planning on getting him to ask you out anyway."

She stares at me, the corner of her mouth turning up. "Really?"

"Yep."

"He's hot. That one."

"Ew. That's my brother you're talking about."

She shrugs. "You're my bestie so I get to tell you everything. Including how hot your brother is."

"Gag."

She slides off the bed and puts the nail polish back in her bag. "I'm gonna let you rest for a bit since I've been in here all morning. I'll see you in a little bit, okay?"

"Okay." I smile, but I really don't want her to go. It's so lonely here, stuck in a stupid, uncomfortable hospital bed with nothing but soap operas on TV. "Thanks for the pretty toes." She reaches out to cover them with the blanket, but I shake my head. "Leave them. They're cute."

"Of course they're cute." She smiles and heads across the room, but as she reaches for the door, it opens. My eyes grow wide at the person who enters, and my stomach flips.

Cole.

Kelsie gives him a quick hello, shoots me a look, and leaves us alone.

He lingers by the door for a second, his eyes on me only. "Can I come in?"

I can't talk, so I nod.

He walks over to the bed and pulls a chair next to it before sitting down. He reaches for my hand, but I pull it away. It takes him a second to recover from that rejection, but his eyes don't leave mine.

"You didn't come," I whisper.

He sighs. "I know."

"Why?"

He hesitates a moment before running a hand through his dark hair. He leans forward after that, reaching for my hand again. "Truth. You scared the crap out of me, Emmy."

My chest hurts again and I take slow deep breaths to calm myself. "Cole, I'm sor—"

"No. I don't want you to apologize for anything. You didn't do anything. It was all me. When I saw you trapped in the car, I . . . freaked. I've had nightmares about it. About you screaming my name and me not being able to help you." He takes a shaky breath. "I couldn't get you out. I'm so sorry. And then I didn't know how bad you were hurt until I saw you lying on the stretcher. You were so . . . broken." He puts his head in his hands and shakes his head. After a second, he looks up, his eyes shining with tears. "I'm sorry. I'm so sorry this happened to you. You of all people don't deserve this."

I let his words sink in and bite my lip to keep from crying, too. "Cole, I'm going to be okay."

"But your legs." He glances at my legs and I squeeze his hand so he'll look at me again.

"My legs are okay." I glance down at my toes and wiggle them again. They're getting stronger. "See?"

"What?" A tear trails down his cheek, and my lip quivers. I never would have thought Cole Evans shed tears. Let alone in front of me. "You can feel them?" he whispers.

"Yes." It's all I can say. I clear my throat to stop the emotion rushing in.

He squeezes my hand so hard it hurts, but I don't break the contact. "I thought . . ." He lets out a slow breath and shakes his head. "I'm so . . ." He sniffs and wipes away more tears. "You're going to walk again?"

"They said I have a good enough diagnosis that I *might* walk again. And you know how stubborn I am. I *will* walk again. And . . ." I swallow the lump in my throat and meet his eyes. "I don't care how hard it is to get there, but I'll ride again, too." My voice cracks on the last word and a tear slips out. "I'm going to ride again so my mom can see me race. She always wanted to see me race, and I want her to be able to see me before . . . before her disease takes over." I close my eyes and take a few breaths to calm my racing heart. "I'm going to walk again for *her*. I don't want her last memories to be of me in a wheelchair."

He nods and brushes his lips against the back of my hand. "If anyone can do it, you can." He glances at me, emotion still swimming in his eyes. "I know you can." I smile as he leans forward and gives me a quick kiss. "And just so you know, I'm not leaving you. I'm with you one hundred percent. I didn't come this far to turn around and leave when things get tough. I want to be with you, Em."

I blink. He wants to be with me. He's not Lucas. He'll never be Lucas, but he's Cole. My Cole. "Good."

He smiles and touches my cheek. The small gesture is so tender I want to cry all over again. "We need each other. You and me. Truths and all."

"Yes. We do."

"Also, I need someone around to fix my bike when it has problems."

"So, that's all you need me for, huh?"

He chuckles. "Mostly." He glances at my toes. "Those are . . . nice, Marty. Real nice."

"So it's Marty again, huh?"

"One more time. For old time's sake."

"Right." We laugh as the door opens and my family plus Kelsie files into the hospital room. Mom holds an In-N-Out bag, and I start salivating as soon as the amazing smell hits me.

"Looks like you were right, Gav," Dad says as he looks at Gavin and winks.

I frown. "About what?"

Gavin walks over and claps Cole on the back. "We knew Cole and Kelsie would be here, so we brought some extra food."

"So does that mean you're not mad if I hold your sister's hand?" Cole asks.

Gavin's eyes narrow on our hands, and then he shrugs. "As long as she doesn't care if I ask out her best friend."

I can't help the grin spreading across my face. "Ask away."

"Already done." He smiles, though he looks embarrassed.

Kelsie beams next to him and doesn't look embarrassed at all.

As I look around at my family and my friends, I feel at peace. Everything's going to be okay. Even if it will take me a while to recover. Even if Mom loses more and more of herself. Her memories and thoughts. We're going to be okay. Because after all is said and done, we'll be together. We need each other. We're stronger together. We're family, after all. And I've never been so proud about that truth in my entire life.

EPILOGUE

The cool breeze caresses my skin as I stare out into the valley below. I pull my knees up to my chest and breathe in the scent of pine from the trees surrounding my spot. This moment right here. Right this second. It's perfect.

Cole brushes some loose strands of hair away from my face and I close my eyes and lean into him as he wraps his arms around me, marveling again at how perfect this moment is.

I never thought I'd be able to come here again, but after a year of intense physical therapy and training, I'm here. I'm back. I'm me again.

Mostly.

I think back on my year and remember all the small successes I've made. Stand with help for one minute. Stand without help for one minute. Take two steps. Take five. Walk across the room. Walk at graduation. Get on a bike and ride down the driveway and back.

I've done them all. Though, it's taken time. And I'll never ever be the same, physically, as I was before the accident, but I'm okay with that. I'm happy and alive. That's what matters.

"You ready to head back down yet?" Cole asks.

I shake my head as he kisses my temple, sending goose bumps over my skin. "Just give me a few more minutes. Then we can go."

He chuckles and settles his chin on the top of my head. "I'm not complaining." He squeezes me tight. "It's nice up here today."

"I know." I sigh and spread my legs in front of me. The legs I thought would never work again. "I love it."

"And I love *you*," he says, kissing my temple again.

I smile and lean into him. So much has changed. I'm in love with a boy who loves me back. I've finally let Lucas go, though he'll always be a part of my life. A part of *me*. You never forget your first love.

Cole kisses the top of my head. "Kelsie's gonna kill us if we're late, you know. She made me swear I'd get you back on time."

I think of my best friend and Gavin, waiting at the bowling alley for us. "I know."

He chuckles. "You get to suffer her wrath then."

"It was your idea to go for a quick ride in the first place."

"I merely suggested it. You're the one who put your bike on the car."

He's right, but I won't admit it that easily. "You're the one who talked me into it. And you know I can't resist a good bike ride."

"I've noticed."

"You ready for your race tomorrow?"

I nod. "My mom's coming. It will be the first race she's ever seen me ride in. Cool, huh?"

"Yep. She'll be proud of you, I'm sure."

"I hope so."

Mom's still not perfect, but she's not worse either. It may be a long time before she gets there, but I'll relish every moment I have with her until that day comes. I promised myself I'd never shut her out again.

"All right. Let's get out of here." I turn around and slide off the rock, wobbling as my feet touch the ground. My right foot is still a little weaker than my left, but it's something I'm going to have to deal with. Maybe for the rest of my life.

"I could have helped you down," Cole says, jumping into the dirt next to me.

"I know. You know me."

"Miss Stubborn." He kisses the tip of my nose and grabs my hand, pulling me toward our bikes leaning against the tree.

A sight so normal now that I smile at the scene.

Cole puts his helmet on and reaches to hook my chin strap together. He leans in, hovering centimeters away from my lips. I close my eyes, waiting for the kiss, but I feel a breeze as he pulls away. I open my eyes and he's jumping on his bike, grinning as he clips his shoes into the pedals. "Race you down!" he says and takes off down the trail.

"No fair! You can't distract me like that!" I jump on my bike, clip my shoes in, and push myself to catch him. Switching gears is second nature to me now, and when I see the next climb, however tough it may be, I'm always going to be ready.

ACKNOWLEDGMENTS

First off, this book wouldn't be where it is today without my wonderful agent, Nicole Resciniti. Thank you so much for your wonderful advice, your faith in me, and all of your hard work getting my books in front of editors. You are the best advocate I could ever ask for.

To my editor, Nicole Frail, for your editing awesomeness and wonderful insights. Thank you for making this book stronger and for still taking a chance on me. It has been a privilege working with you, and our mutual love for The Nightmare Before Christmas is a nice bonus.

To the rest of the Sky Pony team. Thank you for making my book shine and for the beautiful cover. I'm so lucky to have you!

To my readers, Chakell Wardleigh, Chaleese Leishman, Katie Dodge, Ruth Josse, Kim Krey, and Michelle Argyle. Thank you for your wonderful words of wisdom and for always being there to read, no matter how weird or fluffy my books are.

To my amazing writing posse, Katie Dodge, Ruth Josse, Kim Krey, Jeigh Meredith, Donna Nolan, Christene Houston, Suzi Hardy, and Jamie Thompson. Oh, how I love you all. Thank you for the uplifting retreats, the encouragement on bad days, and the love, always. I'd go crazy without you ladies by my side.

To my brother-in-law, Daniel Sedgwick, for answering more medical questions. (This won't be the last time, I'm sure.)

To my wonderful parents, siblings, and in-laws. Thank you for your unfailing love and support in everything I do.

And lastly, to my best friend, my husband, David, whose love of mountain biking inspired a huge part of this story. And to my children, Caden, Kinley, Brooklyn, and Beckam. I love you.